"It's been a while since I've felt like…a woman. I'm a doctor, a pregnant person, I'm a mother-in-waiting. But a woman…"

"Believe me. There's no mistaking the woman." And maybe he'd gone a little too far when he'd kissed her. But he'd been caught up in the moment. Smelled her perfume, held her in his arms, felt her head on his shoulder… He didn't date, didn't have a social life, and Gabrielle was…attractive. More like beautiful. And alone. He was only trying to befriend her, that was all. So the kiss had been a mistake. He'd admit that to himself, and deny its existence to her. Even though she knew he'd kissed her.

But another time, another situation? He could almost picture himself involved with Gabrielle. Maybe even more than involved. She was everything he'd never expected in a woman. Funny, direct, honest, smart. Little Bryce Evans was going to have himself one hell of a mother, and Neil was a little envious he didn't fit into the equation somewhere, because it was a nice equation. One he'd never expected he'd want.

Dear Reader

Welcome to the most idyllic spot I can imagine—White Elk. It's a perfect little village, nestled in the valley between three looming mountain peaks called The Three Sisters by the locals. The people are friendly, the village is picturesque and, according to Indian lore, The Three Sisters protect everyone within their shadows.

Does White Elk exist? In a sense, yes. My husband's parents retired to a place much as I envision White Elk to be. It's lovely. The people there smile at strangers and welcome them in. And the mountains… I love to stand in the valley and look up at them, but, more than that, I love to go up to the various peaks and look out across the valley. I'm a city girl. I'll admit it. But when I write these books I rarely set them in the city because I love to escape, just for a little while. I hope you love your visit to the little village of White Elk as much as I did!

Wishing you health and happiness!

Dianne Drake

PS I love to hear from my readers. Please visit my website at www.DianneDrake.com. Also, feel free to e-mail me at Dianne@DianneDrake.com, and tell me about the places in this world you love.

The second of Dianne's
Mountain Village Hospital stories,

HIS MOTHERLESS LITTLE TWINS,

is also available this month
from Mills & Boon® Medical™ Romance

NEWBORN NEEDS A DAD

BY
DIANNE DRAKE

MILLS & BOON

First published in Great Britain 2010
Harlequin Mills & Boon Limited,
Eton House, 18-24 Paradise Road, Richmond, Surrey TW9 1SR

© Dianne Despain 2010

ISBN: 978 0 263 21495 6

Harlequin Mills & Boon policy is to use papers that are natural,
renewable and recyclable products and made from wood grown in
sustainable forests. The logging and manufacturing process conform
to the legal environmental regulations of the country of origin.

Printed and bound in Great Britain
by CPI Antony Rowe, Chippenham, Wiltshire

Now that her children have left home, **Dianne Drake** is finally finding the time to do some of the things she adores—gardening, cooking, reading, shopping for antiques. Her absolute passion in life, however, is adopting abandoned and abused animals. Right now Dianne and her husband Joel have a little menagerie of three dogs and two cats, but that's always subject to change. A former symphony orchestra member, Dianne now attends the symphony as a spectator several times a month and, when time permits, takes in an occasional football, basketball or hockey game.

Recent titles by the same author:

FOUND: A MOTHER FOR HIS SON
DR VELASCOS' UNEXPECTED BABY
THE WIFE HE'S BEEN WAITING FOR
A BOSS BEYOND COMPARE

CHAPTER ONE

WHAT a beautiful little village! Dr Gabrielle Evans breathed a sigh of relief, shutting off her car in the parking spot marked *Guests*, in front of the quaint White Elk Lodge. She'd lived in large cities too many years. Indoctrinated herself to fast pace and convenience. Nothing about the village called White Elk seemed fast, or convenient and, right now, that suited her just fine. She was tired and, physically, she needed this stop. Surprisingly, it seemed right for her emotionally, too. Even if only for a night. Maybe two, if the bed was comfortable, the food good, a fire in the fireplace inviting, because she did have just the slightest backache, she was hungry, and the mood to settle in and be cozy was dropping down over her like a soft blanket. So much so she could picture herself sitting in front of a great stone fireplace, feet up, dozing off from pure contentment.

Nesting. Which was to be expected in her condition.

Besides, hadn't she seen a little boutique on Main Street, one with the name Handmade for Baby? That was all the excuse she needed for a short holiday here. That, and her swollen ankles. Pregnant-swollen was what she called it when her patients had the same problem. Pregnant-swollen ankles, pregnant-swollen belly. *Not to worry*, she would say. *It's a temporary condition.*

Well, temporary condition or not, she felt like stopping. Something about White Elk appealed to her sense of esthetics. It was a homey little town, its narrow streets lined with pine trees and old-fashioned streetlamps, and white picket fences surrounded the cottage homes she'd seen from her car on the way in. Cottage homes…she'd always wanted to live in a cottage. All in all, everything she'd seen so far in this Alpine-styled village was the antithesis of her steel-and-chrome condo back in Chicago, where she lived in the middle of a mixed residential and industrial area, overlooking a frantic, elevated railway on one side and the bumper-to-bumper Chicago interstate system on the other. Her wake-up call in the morning was the honking of agitated motorists trying to inch their way through impossible traffic and her lullaby at night was the clacking of the old train over the el rails.

And here in White Elk…no traffic. Just a few lazy drivers on the street, none who seemed agitated, none who seemed in a hurry. That, alone, could have been an enticement to stay over, if everything else she could see around her hadn't already drawn her in. Besides, the drive back to the airport was still another ninety miles, and her reservation home to Chicago wasn't until tomorrow. Meaning she was going to stay in a hotel room for the night somewhere. So, why not here? "And it's not like I've got anything to hurry back to," she said aloud, a habit she'd developed since she'd learned she was pregnant. Talking to her unborn baby…it's what she urged her patients to do, and in this case, she took her own advice. Chattered away to him all the time. "Anyway, what's the hurry getting back? It's not like I have a job waiting for me any more. Right now, I'm here, and here seems very nice. You should see it, Bryce. People smile. Perfect strangers wave."

Yes, a night or two here was exactly what the pregnant doctor needed, which was why she prescribed it for herself.

Gabby pulled out her cell phone and dialed the number posted under the wooden, hand-carved Welcome sign nailed to a lodgepole. It was a lazy thing to do, but all of a sudden she felt like being a little lazy. After the day she'd had, she deserved some laziness and a nice cup of hot chocolate on top of that! "Hello," she said, when the woman who called herself Laura Stewart answered the phone. "I was wondering if you have a room available for one night." She glanced across the street and discovered the little shop White Elk Confectionary, specializing in *chocolate*. Fate? "Maybe two nights," she added, because she really did want that chocolate. Sure, it was almost spring—technically spring had sprung a few days ago, but there was still snow on the ground here, in patchy spots, so in Gabby's mind she was allowed her craving for hot chocolate. "One person," she added. Well, almost two.

According to Laura, there were plenty of rooms available, so Gabby crawled out of her rental car, stretched her aching back, decided not to look down in the inevitable lost cause of locating her puffy ankles, which she couldn't see now anyway, and forced herself *not* to waddle when she walked inside, although several friends back home had recently commented on her waddling.

"That didn't take long," the friendly-looking strawberry blonde at the desk said as Gabby dropped her overnight bag on the floor and her purse on the desk.

"I was just outside. Called from the parking lot. These days, if I can find a way to be lazy, I do it." She smiled. "Actually, I look for ways to be lazy and the more pregnant I get, the lazier I want to be."

"Don't blame you. Been in your condition three times myself, and if ever there's a time to be pampered…"

If there was someone there to pamper you, Gabby thought, her eyes going immediately to Laura's ring finger. A simple gold band there said it all. She had someone to pamper her, where Gabby did not. But that was fine because, normally, she didn't need pampering. In fact, she prided herself on her independence.

"Is this your first?" Laura continued.

Instinctively, Gabby laid her hand on her belly. Yes, her first. Unexpected. Very welcomed. "Yes, it is," she said, not really sure she wanted to go any further. People reacted differently to her situation and it wasn't a matter of feeling awkward in her very pregnant, very unmarried condition so much as it was that she didn't want to make people feel awkward around her. She was a medical doctor, she knew how these kinds of things happened, and in a moment of weakness, well, it had happened to her. No excuses, no apologies. "And I saw a lovely little baby shop down the street. I thought I might go take a look after I'm rested. I haven't really started baby shopping yet."

"You haven't?" Laura seemed genuinely surprised. "I think I was out buying baby bootees about ten minutes after the test strip confirmed my pregnancy…with my first. With my second it took about an hour, and with my third about a day." She glanced down at Gabby's belly. "I'm surprised you could hold off this long."

It wasn't so much that she was holding off as it was she was scared to make plans. "Oh, I've figured that I'd probably do a big binge shop when the time comes. You know, go crazy, buy everything in the store. But I haven't had time." And she'd had patients who'd put all their hopes and dreams into a miracle baby, like hers, only to be heartbroken. Even though she had only two months to go, she wasn't ready to invest herself in so many hopes. "Who knows, maybe Handmade for Baby will be the lucky recipient of all my saved-up baby-shopping urges once I'm rested."

Laura laughed. "Janice Laughlin will love you forever. She's the owner. Anyway, speaking of getting rested, I think we should get you to your room. The ski season's over now, except for a few brave souls who hang around hoping for late snow. So, you can have your choice of rooms—one here in the lodge—something small, a large suite. Or you can have a cabin all to yourself."

"You have cabins?" That sounded like the coziness she wanted. "With a fireplace?"

"With a fireplace."

A cabin with a fireplace in a ski-resort community, baby shopping, hot chocolate... Suddenly, Gabby was looking forward to her next couple of days. It was like this was exactly the place she was meant to be. Yes, nesting. Her patients talked about it all the time—finding the place you wanted to be, settling in, dwelling on your pregnancy. Now, for the first time, she believed she understood what that meant, and if this was, indeed, nesting, it agreed with her because she wasn't feeling so bleak, so alone, like she had too many times these past months. "A cabin... Yes, I'd love a cabin with a fireplace."

"It's a little bit of a hike to get up there," Laura warned. "Not steep, but not so convenient to the parking lot as the lodge is."

"In spite of the obvious, I'm in good shape. Just a little tired right now because I've been on the road for a while, and I *really* hate traveling. Generally, though, I'm active and a nice walk back and forth will do me some good." Especially now that she didn't get all the exercise she had when she'd worked every day.

"Good. But I still don't want you lifting anything heavy, so I'll have my daughter carry your bags up to the cabin when she gets home from school in a couple of hours..."

Gabby shook her head. "Not necessary. All I have is an overnighter, and I can carry it myself. I didn't expect to be staying so I didn't bring much with me." Actually, she wasn't sure what she *had* expected when she'd set out on this trip. A quick announcement to Gavin Thierry, letting him know he was about to become a father, then a quick retreat? Certainly she hadn't expected much from him. After all, there'd been no lasting relationship. But to find out what she had... "Thanks, anyway, for offering."

Laura spun around the register for Gabby to sign, then handed her the cabin key when the paperwork was completed. "We have a dining room here, but if you'd like..." she took a look at the name on the register "...*Gabrielle*, I can have someone bring dinner to your cabin later on."

"Call me Gabby." Her father had been the only one ever to call her Gabrielle, and hearing someone else call her by that name now hurt. "And I appreciate the offer, but I'd rather come down to the dining room, if it's all the same to you. I think getting out, keeping myself active, is a good idea." As an obstetrician, it's what she prescribed for her patients. Then scolded them when they didn't take her advice.

"Well, if you need anything, call the main switch. Oh, and so you'll know, we do have a small hospital in the village, not that I think anything will happen. But to be on the safe side in case, well...you know...there's the White Elk Hospital, and it's pretty nice. Very good in general services for adults and, believe it or not, well known for its pediatric practices. And what we lack in big-town medical services we make up for in some very nice, very competent doctors and nurses."

Glowing praise that intrigued her, and she caught herself wondering what it would be like working in a small town like White Elk. And raising her son here. "Well, I'm not due yet, so let's hope I won't be needing any medical care while I'm here."

Wasn't this what she wanted? A fresh start, someplace other than a large, impersonal city like Chicago? That's what she'd told herself when she'd sold her share of the medical practice to her partners and, just last week, had started the process of putting her condo on the market with the expectation of finding someplace else to start her new life. She was looking for something different, something she wasn't quite able to define. That's what she kept telling herself, anyway. What it was or where it would be were still great big questions, but she trusted that she would know it when she saw it.

Could it be White Elk? The feel was right, it was definitely different from what she'd had, but it was also so small. Moving here from Chicago would be a huge culture shock and with all the other drastic changes going on in her life now, she wasn't sure she should even think about one like this. White Elk had nice shops and a bed in a cozy cabin for a night but, generally, she liked a few more amenities around her, and a few more luxuries. This was a place where you spent a nice holiday, but to settle here?

Crazy thoughts. Pregnancy thoughts—a combination of hormones, flailing emotions over the news of her baby's father's death, and a whole lot of uncertainty. That's what it had to be. Her thinking was a little skew these days as she had someone else to consider now, and her decisions didn't affect only her. Besides, she needed to work, needed to settle somewhere the red carpet was out for an obstetrician, and what were the odds of that happening here?

"To get to your cabin, go out behind the lodge, take the first trail to the left, and I've got you in the first one you'll come to. It's got the best view of the Three Sisters."

"Three sisters?"

"Our three mountain peaks. They overlook the valley and, according to Indian legend, take care of the people who live here. Of course, we have busy ski resorts on each of the peaks now, which is what has made White Elk thrive." She smiled. "Tourists. We love them to pieces here."

"With so many tourists I'd say the Three Sisters are doing what they're supposed to." Watching and protecting…the very same things she did for this baby she'd be delivering in a while. The same things she wished she had someone to do for her, which simply wasn't in her future.

The hike to the cabin was pleasant, the air cool and brisk, but not as cold as it could have been for the last week of March. Along the trail, little purple and yellow crocuses poked their heads out of the remnants of the last snow, giving Gabby the hope that the full burst of spring was just around the corner. By the time that happened, she'd be a mother, settled in wherever she was supposed to be. "A mother," she said, simply to remind herself. Sometimes she still couldn't believe it. This little boy inside her was a dream coming true in a way she'd have never expected in a million years. Of course, now that she knew of Gavin's death, she was a little sad. They hadn't been romantically involved. Outside of what she'd seen of him as a doctor, she hadn't even known him well enough to tell her son what kind of person his father had been other than smart, kind, considerate. Bryce did deserve to know, but what could she say? *Your mother was feeling very lonely, and very vulnerable when she met a pleasant, handsome man at a medical symposium, spent a night with him and conceived you as a result.*

Unfortunately, that's all there was to the story. It had taken her weeks to find Gavin, and weeks to get up the courage to come tell him what had happened that one night they'd spent together. But by then it had been too late. Meaning there was nothing to add to the story and Bryce would never know his father. Gavin had no family in Spotswood, where'd she'd just visited. None that she could find. And no one there who could tell her about his family either. Sad for her son, sad for her.

Gabby stopped for a moment, and thought about picking a few of the flowers for her cabin, but decided to leave them as they were, a tiny bit of inspiration fighting against the elements. "You know we're going to be fine," she said to her unborn baby. "It's just a little tough right now. I wanted you to know about him and I'm sorry I didn't find him sooner. But we'll work it out, just you and me, and I promise that if there's any information available about him…" Information, but no father.

It wasn't like she was afraid of raising a baby as a single mother, because she wasn't. In fact, from the instant she'd discovered she was pregnant, she'd been shocked, excited, scared, in awe after a lifetime being told, and believing, it wouldn't ever happen to her, that she could not get pregnant. She'd been injured in a riding accident years ago. Too much scar tissue, the doctors had said soon after. Too little hope. When she'd been fifteen, that hadn't really had much of an impact on her. When she'd turned thirty, it had. But she'd lived with it, accepted it.

Then, after all those years of believing, as the patient, and even as a doctor, that nothing could happen, she'd had the recurring feeling that maybe, just maybe she might be pregnant. Missed period one month and she'd convinced herself it was stress, that her job was demanding. Missed period the second month and she'd gone to the local pharmacy for a home pregnancy kit, then had sat it on the bathroom countertop and stared at it for three days before she'd opened it. After that she'd waited another two days before she'd actually gotten around to using it. Then, when that test strip had gone from pink to blue, she'd run, not walked, but *run* to the corner pharmacy, bought another kit, done another test. Then gone back to that same pharmacy one more time, one more kit.

A kindly pharmacist who'd seen her grabbing yet another test kit off the shelf had suggested she go see an obstetrician, and offered to make a referral if she needed one. But she was an obstetrician, and a very pregnant one, she was coming to realize. Also a very overwhelmed one. "Right now, your only problem is that your mother's very tired. But I'm on my way to fix that situation immediately."

Bryce Evans. Her miracle baby. She couldn't wait for his arrival into the world. Nothing other than that really mattered. And she was so happy…

"Thanks for making a house call. We're not busy right now, but with David out of town, it's like I'm doing the work of a dozen different people and there aren't enough hours in the day to get everything done that needs to be."

Dr Neil Ranard handed the bottle of pink bubble-gum-tasting liquid over to Laura. They called it bubble-gum tasting, and he'd successfully convinced a number of his young patients that was the case, but to him it tasted like…medicine. Nasty, nasty medicine. "Just give her the dose listed on the label and she'll be fine. There's a sore throat bug going around the elementary school and Emily is one of the many. Also I'll want to check her again in a couple of days, but she'll be ready to come to the clinic by then." Yes, he still made house calls. In a small town, that was possible, and he really liked getting back to personal medicine. Two years away had taught him so many things, but the biggest lesson learnt was that everything he needed was here. He was a small-town doctor, and that's exactly what he wanted to be.

"Can you stay for dinner, Neil? I have only a handful of paying guests checked in right now, and I'm making enough food for an army. Can't get out of the habit of cooking for a lodge full of people when the season shuts down, I guess."

"Wish I could, but I really should get back. With Walt Graham retired now, and Eric Ramsey being tied up with the twins—they're both down with sore throats—we're a little short-handed in emergency. And I've still got a few appointments to take care of at the clinic before I go make hospital rounds. But thanks. I appreciate the offer." At the White Elk Hospital and Clinic, he was the pediatrician, but family practice was also his responsibility, as well as covering Emergency when it was necessary, and doing the occasional mountain rescue. It was a varied job, and in such a small setting every doctor was called on to do pretty much whatever they had to. Medical convention aside, he loved it. Where else would he be so fortunate as to be involved in so many things?

"Can't you wait five minutes, while I get something together to send back with you? It's better than what you'll get at the hospital, and you know hospital food is what you'll end up eating." She grinned. "Think about it, Neil. Institutional cooking versus home cooking."

Home cooking, a luxury he hadn't even had those months he'd been married. It sounded good, actually. *Anything* resembling a normal life sounded good. Otherwise, for him it *would* be whatever the hospital cafeteria special was. "OK, you've convinced me. Mind if I go sit in the dining room and pour myself a cup of coffee while I wait?"

Laura dismissed Neil with the wave of an unconcerned hand, and he ambled into the empty dining room, went straight to the service bar and poured his coffee, then took a seat by the window that gave him the best view of the Three Sisters. Magnificent view, and one he had so little time to admire these days. It was also the view that had drawn him back home, even when he'd vowed, almost three years ago, not to return. But he'd returned, in part because he liked skiing when he had the time. And the fresh air. Most of all, he liked the nice people. All that, and the exciting nature of his medical practice. Here, in White Elk, he had it all. Or most of it. Because the memories of his short-lived marriage were here, too. As were the memories of the day his wife had run off with his brother.

But the good outweighed the bad. That's what he kept telling himself and maybe someday he'd even convince himself of it, because some of the memories were bitter. And forever unresolved.

Neil stretched out his long legs and leaned back in the wooden chair, trying to empty his mind of everything. Movement at the opposite end of the dining room caught his attention, though…attention in the form of one very pretty, very pregnant woman who was sizing up the various tables, obviously looking for one with the best view.

He studied her for a moment. She looked almost lonely, ambling from table to table the way she was, all by herself. And here he was, occupying the one with the view he knew she had to be looking for. Immediately, Neil sprang to his feet, and even thought to motion her in his direction, like he was the maître d'. But as he plucked his coffee mug up off the table and stepped away from it, she found her seat on the opposite end of the room, in a spot overlooking the town—all the shops, and the people bustling up and down the sidewalks.

Funny, he thought, how people had different ideas of what was perfect. Personally, his idea of perfect went to something wild, something without people. Hers went to just the opposite, it seemed.

"Your dinner, Neil," Laura said, setting the brown paper bag full of plastic containers in front of him. "There should be enough to get you through the next couple of days, and if there's not, come back. There's always more where that came from."

"Appreciate the home cooking," he replied absently, unable

to take his stare off the woman, who was now seated with her back to him.

Laura, noticing his intent stare, smiled. "She checked in several hours ago," she whispered. "Not from around here. She registered her home address as Chicago and I don't know a thing about her other than that." She paused, then chuckled. "Except the obvious."

"And that she looks lonely," he commented out loud, although he'd meant the remark to stay in his head.

"You know, she did look a little lonely, come to think of it. I thought she was mostly tired, though." Laura shrugged it off as she scurried over to the other table to take Gabby's dinner order, while Neil stayed there, sipping his coffee, watching a while longer than he really should have, given his schedule.

Strangers came to town all the time. In fact, the town's economy was built on people coming here to stay for a while, whether to ski, or shop, or simply have a nice holiday. He barely even noticed them unless they had a medical problem. So what was it about this woman that caught his attention...not only caught it, but held it?

Nothing, he said to himself. Absolutely nothing at all. Right now, he didn't get involved. Not with anyone. He was married to his work, and he owned a part interest in a hospital. That was enough to keep him out of trouble, keep him fairly contented, keep him reasonably happy. Life was good. Why try for anything else?

Thinking about what had happened the last time he'd tried for something different was what propelled him back to his feet, and carried him right out the door. When he got to the entrance, though, Neil stopped and turned back to look at her, and that's when he saw her face. She was...beautiful. Stunning. Honey-blond hair falling gracefully to her shoulders, her blue eyes cast downward. Almost shyly...eyes that could only have been blue. And perfect lips. He was observing her as a physician, of course. Only as a physician.

She was what that pregnant glow was all about. He wasn't sure he'd ever truly seen it before, but now that he'd seen her, he knew what it looked like.

In that brief moment when his eyes were still fixed on her, she glanced up at him, stared outright for a long moment, then looked away. That's when Neil knew he'd better leave before good judgment was overcome with something he didn't understand, and he intruded where he clearly wasn't wanted. But once outside on the walkway, he looked back up to the window where she sat, and…was she staring at him? It seemed she might have been.

Handsome face. Rugged. Nice firm jaw, nice straight nose. With his wavy black hair, she imagined dark brown eyes. Or green. No…they had to be dark brown.

It was a face that should have been familiar, but nothing in her memory could place him. His eyes haunted her, though. So familiar. But she didn't often forget a man so handsome. Yet in that span of mere seconds, when their gazes had crossed, it had been like she'd been looking into eyes she'd looked into before. The same, yet not.

Just pregnancy hormones kicking in. Still, at first glance, he'd seemed so familiar. Then, at second glance, he didn't at all. His was one of those faces that would plague her for a while, though, until she placed him, or forgot him.

"Who was that?" she asked Laura, as Laura placed the handwritten menu on the table in front of her. Potato, vegetable and salad choices were the same with every meal, and she had her choice of meat, poultry or fish.

"Neil Ranard. He owns the family practice clinic at the hospital. And, actually, he's part owner of the hospital.

Specializes in pediatrics, but all the docs there do a little bit of everything."

Would she have known him from some medical event—a seminar they'd both attended, perhaps? Or maybe a medical convention?

In theory, that sounded good, except she rarely ever had time for seminars, and as for medical conventions… She'd been to exactly one, and it hadn't been the White Elk doctor she'd fixed herself on there. So that left… Honestly, she didn't know. And she didn't want to keep thinking about it. "I think I'd like the vegetables only, if you don't mind. Bryce and I don't seem to do so well with meat these days."

"Bryce?"

Gabby laughed, self-conscious. "My baby. I'm going to name him Bryce, and I guess I'm getting in the habit of using his name. Thinking of him as a person." She'd been in the habit from the moment she'd known she was pregnant. It was going to be a boy, and she would name him Bryce after her father, a decision made the instant she'd thrown away the third pregnancy kit. Bryce…that was the only way she could make sense of things.

Laura laughed. "Boys are nice. At least, that's what I've heard. We've got three girls, and I'm not sure if I'd know what to do with a boy now, after so many years."

"To be honest, I'm not sure I'm going to know what to do with a baby, boy or girl."

"You're…alone?" Laura asked, hesitant.

"Well, I was until about seven months ago." Noncommittal response that would suffice. Smiling, she patted her belly. "But that's sure not the case now."

"I talked to my girls too…in the womb. Read books to them, sang to them, played music for them. My husband thought I was crazy, but for the whole time I was pregnant, I wasn't alone, and I needed to make that connection." She shrugged. "Anyway, I'd better get back to the kitchen."

Once Laura was gone, Gabby turned her attention back to the window, wondering if she'd see the man, Neil Ranard, again, but he was gone. Oh, well...

"I'll take both of them." Two quilts weren't too many, and both were so adorable. So were the fifteen newborn outfits she'd bought, along with the crib accessories, the bootees, the hats... There were so many baby things she'd never thought about before and, so far, she'd bought every single thing she'd looked at. This morning her ankles were normal, her back felt fine, Bryce was kicking up a storm, and she was totally in love with Handmade for Baby. It was an amazing little store, fronted on the main street right next to a candy store. She hadn't been in there yet, but she would. And she intended to browse through the little maternity boutique that Debbi Laughlin, the baby-store clerk, had recommended.

"You staying here long?" Debbi asked. She was seventeen at most, with short, spiky yellow hair, a pierced eyebrow, and an engaging, warm smile.

"Just another day, then I'll be going back to Chicago."

Debbi arched her eyebrows over the mention of Chicago and Gabby's gaze fixed on the little silver ring anchored there that bobbed up and down. "I've always wanted to go there. Maybe even save my money and move there, go to college...anywhere but here."

"You don't like it here?" Gabby asked. So far, she hadn't found anything in White Elk she didn't like.

"It's OK, if you're old, I suppose."

Old, like she was? Gabby laughed inwardly at the thought. Thirty-three wasn't old, but to someone Debbi's age, it was ancient. "Well, I think it's a nice little town."

"Little's the thing. I don't like little. It's boring."

And Gabby didn't like big any more, but she supposed she'd have thought a small town was the end of the world when she'd been younger. She and her dad had always lived in a big city—Chicago, New York, San Francisco—and that's what she knew. *All she knew.* But those pregnancy hormones were changing her in ways she hadn't expected, for now her ideal seemed just the opposite of Debbi's and in some ways the opposite of the ones she'd become comfortable with in herself until she'd gotten pregnant. "Well, then, you'd like Chicago, because there's nothing little about it."

"What do you do there?" Debbi asked, as she folded the first quilt into a box.

"I'm an obstetrician. That means—"

"I know what it means. My uncle's a doctor here."

Was she related to Neil Ranard? "Dr Ranard?"

Debbi shook her head. "Dr Ramsey. He works with Dr Ranard when the twins aren't sick. Which they are right now, which is why I'm here and my mother isn't. She's helping Uncle Eric."

"Twins?"

"My cousins. Both of them down with a sore throat and I told my uncle I wasn't going anywhere near them, so my mother's there helping take care of them and I'm here, doing this."

And not loving it, Gabby thought. Too bad. Life was too short not to love what you were doing.

Debbi folded the second quilt into another box, then sat it in the stack with at least fifteen other boxes. "So, did you come to take over for Doc Graham?"

"Who's Doc Graham?"

Debbi blew a bubble with her gum, then popped it. "The obstetrician. He retired so he could have more time to hike, and go skiing. If it were me, I'd retire and get out of here."

"No. I'm not here to replace Doc Graham. I'm just traveling through, and decided to stop and do some shopping."

Debbi nodded, but the expression on her face showed that she thought Gabby was crazy for intentionally staying in White Elk when she didn't have to. "So, what do you want me to do with all this stuff?" she asked.

Good question. Gabby hadn't thought that far ahead, and her first response was to give Debbi the address to her Chicago condo and have every last thing shipped there. But for some reason she didn't understand, she decided instead to have it sent back to her cabin at the lodge and figure out what to do with it later. Farewells with Debbi were brief, but she felt compelled to tell the girl to look her up if she ever made it to Chicago. Debbi's response was to roll her eyes, plug the earpieces back into her ears and listen to some tune Gabby was sure she'd never heard of.

Next, she visited the candy shop, then the maternity boutique, sending more packages back to her cabin from both shops, as well as stopping at the corner toy store and showing amazing restraint by buying only one stuffed teddy bear and a little wooden train set Bryce wouldn't play with for years. Shopping done, she felt amazingly good. Refreshed. Full of energy. So she wandered down the street, in the direction of the hospital. Deliberately.

What a cute hospital! Not at all institutional-looking, like where she'd worked back in Chicago. That was a real brick-and-mortar structure, nine stories tall, spanning several blocks, if you included the various clinics and asphalted parking lots. This hospital was quaint, made of logs, resembling a mountain lodge more than it did a hospital. If not for the sign out front indicating that it was, indeed, White Elk Hospital, she would have walked right on by, looking for a more regular-looking institution.

So, she was there. Wondering what came next. "Maybe I'm crazy," she whispered to herself. "But if they do need an obstetrician…" That's what Debbi, the store clerk, had implied. But why had she deliberately come here? To apply for the job? No way. Quaint was nice for a visit, and while she wasn't big-city obsessed like Debbi, she was reasonably sure that she agreed with the girl on the fact that White Elk was too small.

But here she was anyway. It must have been the nesting thing again. Had to be. More rushing hormones telling her to settle down, make a real home for this baby, and White Elk Village was a nice candidate for all those things. Except the idea was ridiculous. Her opportunities here would be too limited. Besides, nobody needed a seven-months-pregnant obstetrician. And at seven months pregnant, the obstetrician didn't really need a full-time job. Money wasn't a problem, but time on her hands was. She did want to work. Loved working, and she already missed it.

"But I've never lived in a city smaller than Chicago," she said to Bryce, "and I'm not sure your mother is cut out for small-town living." Even though this small town was tugging at her. "And don't go telling me I can make a go of it anywhere I want because I'm not sure I can. There are so many things to consider, like my career, and your education."

"Excuse me? Can I help you with something?"

The sexy, smooth voice startled Gabby out of her mental conundrum, caused her to gasp and grab her belly. She rounded to face him, and caught herself staring into the most gorgeous dark brown eyes she'd ever seen. Dark brown, like she'd thought they should be. Glad they were.

"I thought I heard you say something."

She shook her head. "I was just…taking a walk, trying to get a little exercise, and I think I got myself turned around." Well, that was a bit of a lie as she knew exactly where she was.

"I stopped for a moment to get my bearings and you probably heard me muttering to myself. Bad habit. I do that when I'm nervous." Better to admit that than to tell him she was engaged in a debate with her unborn child, and her unborn child seemed to be winning the argument at the moment. Muttering made her look eccentric, debating with an unborn baby made her look just plain odd.

"You're staying up at Laura's lodge, aren't you? I thought I saw you there last night."

Gabby nodded. "It's up at the top of the hill, isn't it?" she said, pointing in the direction she knew perfectly well. Was that really her, feigning the helpless woman? Good thing she had pregnancy hormones to blame it on, because there wasn't anything helpless about her. Her father had raised her well in that aspect, and she took great pride in her independence.

"It's a pretty long walk, going uphill the whole way. Maybe I could call someone to come get you? A friend, a husband…"

"It's not so bad," she said. "Besides, I'm here by myself."

He glanced at his watch, then at the hospital. "How about I get my car and drive you back? It'll only take five minutes."

This would have been such a nice meeting had she not been pregnant, but she was, so this was only about chivalry. He was a pleasant man coming to the rescue of a damsel who didn't need rescuing. End of story. "Thanks, but I'll walk."

"Then maybe you should come inside and sit down for a few minutes before you attempt going back up." He gestured to the hospital. "Ten minutes. Find a nice, comfortable chair, put your feet up…"

"My doctor thinks I should be a little more active than that. She's of the opinion that healthy, pregnant women should be active women. But like I said, thanks."

"Then I'll walk with you."

"Because I'm pregnant? Are you one of those people who

believes a pregnant woman isn't capable of doing anything? Because if you are…"

He thrust his palm out to stop her. "Whoa, I was only trying to be polite. Something my mother taught me."

"Maybe she should have also taught you that pregnant women can take care of themselves just fine."

He chuckled. Deep, sexy. "Actually, she did. And she'd send me to bed without supper for acting the way I have been." He took a step backwards and thrust out his hand. "Hello, my name is Neil Ranard. Can we start over?"

Gabby took his hand and nodded. "And I'm Gabrielle Evans. People call me Gabby…even the ones who accost me, then try to lecture me on the street."

"Then I'll have to call you Gabrielle so you won't be reminded of this rather inauspicious first meeting. It's nice to meet you, Gabrielle."

Gabrielle…it sounded so nice the way he said it. Sounded almost right and, strangely, she didn't object. Didn't object to the twinkle in his eyes either. Sexy, but mischievous. And, yes, even at her rather advanced stage of pregnancy, those thoughts still did pop into her mind. A good-looking man was a good-looking man and even her whacked-out hormones wouldn't deny that. Neil Ranard was handsome and, like she'd thought yesterday, something about him seemed vaguely familiar. "Do I know you?" she asked. "Have you come to Chicago for any reason lately?" It had to be something in Chicago as until yesterday she hadn't left the city for nearly two years.

"Actually, I've never been to Chicago, outside a layover in the airport, and that was probably five years ago. Maybe six."

"You're not famous, are you? I wouldn't have seen you on television, or in a magazine?" Or on the cover of a romance novel?

"Sorry. I'm only famous in my own mind. And even then, it's highly overrated, if not totally ignored, except by my mother and her sister."

"I guess you've got one of those faces, then," she said, still wondering why she couldn't shake herself of the feeling. "Look, I appreciate you being concerned about me, but I'm fine, and there's no need to help me get back to the lodge."

"What if I said that Laura makes the best cheesecake in White Elk Valley, and you're my excuse to go have a piece?"

"Then I'd say you're a terrible liar. But I appreciate the gesture." With that, Gabby turned and started the climb back up the hill to her cabin. She'd only gone ten steps, though, when she stopped and spun back around. He was right on her heels. "Are you following me?"

"Actually, I thought I'd go to the lodge and have a piece of cheesecake. Talking about it made me hungry for it."

"Liar!" she exclaimed, fighting to control the laugh bubbling up inside her.

He arched playful eyebrows. "I'd never lie about a good piece of cheesecake."

"But you were looking at your watch just a minute ago, which tells me you're in a hurry to get back to work. So you really don't want that cheesecake right now, and you're using it as a pretty lame excuse to make sure I can get myself back up the hill. Which I can do perfectly well without anybody's help."

His face went serious. "I know it's none of my business, but how long has it been since you've seen a doctor, Gabrielle?"

"If I'm not mistaken, I'm looking at one right now."

"I mean an obstetrician."

She smiled. "If I'm not mistaken, *you're* looking at one right now."

"No kidding? You're an obstetrician?"

"No kidding. And if I'm not mistaken, you might be in

need of one here for a few weeks. According to Debbi, at Handmade for Baby."

Obvious surprise blinked across his face. "You're applying for a job?"

"Not really a full-time job. But I could fill in until your new obstetrician arrives. As it turns out, I left my old position a few weeks ago, so I've got the time."

"I've got to admit, you've caught me off guard. We were just having a staff meeting, wondering what we were going to do, and here you are, on our front walk."

As they always said, timing was everything. She hadn't meant to apply for a position, although she'd thought about it. Hadn't meant to stay here in White Elk, although she'd thought about that, too. Yes, after Debbi had mentioned that their former obstetrician had just left, the idea of staying awhile had tempted her. Now here she was, making it happen. "Well, I do come with an obvious condition." She raised her hands to her belly. "Two months to go. But I'm healthy, fit to work, and if you need me for a while…"

"Do we need you? Our obstetrician's been phasing himself out without phasing someone else in to take his place. We thought he had a while to go before he finally left so we weren't too worried, then one morning he woke up and just couldn't do it any more. It was time for him to leave."

Something she understood all too well. That's exactly what had happened to her in Chicago. She'd known she was going, hadn't known when, then one day it had been time. "Well, my credentials will check out, and I can give you some personal references."

"We'll need you for six weeks at the longest. I've got someone else coming in to take over after that, on a temporary basis until we can find someone to fill the full-time position. But we had this big gap between Walt and the temp."

"Six weeks sounds good." So did temporary. And this *was* perfect timing, wasn't it? She could work for six weeks, *part-time*, have her baby after that, and put off trying to figure out, for a while longer, what came next in her life. "Unless something unforeseen and early changes my plans."

"In which case, I'll be glad to deliver your baby."

An offer she could hardly refuse. Pregnant and employed again. If only for a little while for both conditions. She liked it. In fact, she was excited to be working again, and didn't doubt for a minute that she could handle it. So she extended her hand to the incredibly handsome Dr Neil Ranard, and instantly a little chill shot up her arm. "When do I start?" she asked, her hand lingering in his just a fraction of a second longer than it should have.

"Five minutes ago OK with you?"

Reluctantly, she pulled her hand from his and crammed it into her jacket pocket. "Five minutes ago is perfect." Then she shivered again.

Just the chilly air, she told herself. What else could it be?

CHAPTER TWO

WELL, it wasn't a busy schedule. Fallon O'Gara, the nurse practitioner—a bright-eyed woman about Gabby's age, with wild red hair streaming down her back, a wide, cheery smile that came naturally and a laugh that bubbled through the air— handed Gabby a schedule with all of two afternoon patients for her to see. "That's it? Just two?"

"Walt Graham did help in the emergency department when he wasn't busy, but I'm not so sure we should put you on that schedule, too. Neil…Dr Ranard…said he wants you on ob- stetrics only, and I can't change that without his authorization. So, until I hear further, yes, that's it, unless someone else schedules an appointment with you."

"But can I change the schedule if I want to? Or maybe wander down there and put myself to work?" Sitting around all afternoon, twiddling her thumbs, would make her feel useless, and since she was on a campaign to prove that pregnancy in the workplace still had a place, she decided she was going to have to change some minds here. Or, at least, one specific mind.

Fallon laughed. "He warned me that you were a little head-strong. Told me to hold my ground with you."

"Not headstrong. I just like to work." She patted her belly. "*We* like to work."

"Well, Neil wants me to do a physical on you before you start anything. I know you're only a short-time, part-timer, but he's pretty stringent about keeping his staff healthy. And since you're so far along, I think it's best." She thrust out her hand to stop Gabby before she could protest. "I know you're an obste-trician and you know better than any of us how you're feeling and what you can handle, but rules are rules, and like I said…"

"Neil is pretty stringent." Translated to mean thorough. In her estimation, that made him a good doctor.

"On the bright side, if I don't find any problems, I'll bet you can talk him into letting you take your turn in Emergency."

"So let's do this check-up." To be honest, she hadn't had one in a few weeks, and she was due for one. "But can we do it after I see my first patient? It looks like her appointment was thirty minutes ago, and unless another one of your staff has already seen her, I don't want to keep her waiting any longer."

Fallon waved her off when a mother wrestling four little ones came through the door. They were carrying balloons and painted drawings and a vase with flowers, on their way to visit daddy, who was resting comfortably in the orthopedics ward with his leg in traction. Happy, eager, smiling faces… When she'd been young, she'd always said she wanted lots of children when she grew up. Being the only child of a single father, she'd thought a large family would be nice. She still believed that, but she was contented with one child. Elated, actually.

"So, how are you feeling today, Mrs Blanchard?" Angela Blanchard, who was sitting on the edge of the exam table, covered only in a blue paper exam gown, looked…frustrated. Not unhappy, but not happy, either.

"Not as good as you, since you're working and I'm not," she snapped. "Sorry. I'm not having a good day."

"Understandable."

"Is there some way to get this thing delivered early? Induce labor, maybe?"

A quick survey of Angela's chart revealed she was due two weeks after Gabby. She was healthy and there was nothing of alarm going on except, perhaps, her attitude. "Would it make any difference if I said that you're over two thirds of the way there and the rest is downhill from here?"

A laugh broke through Angela's mood. "The one thing I could always count on with Doc Graham was that he would be at least as grumpy as I was. And now I've got a doctor who smiles. Guess that means I have to smile, too, doesn't it?"

"It helps. You ought to try it." Gabby sat the chart aside and extended her hand to Angela. "Hi, I'm Gabby Evans, and I'll be smiling at you for the next few weeks. Five or six, if I'm lucky."

"So we're due almost the same time," Angela responded, taking Gabby's hand. She was a small woman, with short-cropped brown hair and dark brown eyes. Almost a pixie…a pixie with a sizeable tummy spread, side to side.

"Just a few weeks apart, and I know what you mean, wanting to get it over with. There are times I'd really love to see the floor again." She wrapped the blood-pressure cuff around Angela's arm and pumped it up. "Or my ankles. But I guess that comes soon enough, doesn't it?" Then she listened for the dull sound of the blood pressure through her stethoscope. It was high. Not alarmingly so, but enough that Gabby took a second reading to make sure. Again, it registered barely on the high end of normal.

"Did Doc Graham ever diagnose you with hypertension?"

Angela was instantly alarmed. "No, why?"

"You're on the verge. Nothing to worry about yet, but I

want to keep an eye on it. So, do you live far from here?" she asked Angela.

"No, about twenty minutes."

"Good, then I'd like you to stop in tomorrow for another blood-pressure check."

"Should I be nervous about this?"

Gabby shook her head. "Could be nothing. Could be because you're stressing. Of course, even bringing it up puts you under more stress, which could raise your blood pressure. But I want to stay on top of this, keep it under control if it's the start of something, or rule it out if it's not." The only real concern was that, according to Doc Graham's notes, Angela's blood pressure had been normal all along. "And in the meantime, reduce your salt intake, stay away from highly processed foods with a lot of sodium in them, and if you're not walking, walk."

"I walked. In fact, that's all I did until Doc Graham made me quit working. I manage the kitchen up on the older Sister…"

"Older sister?"

"The mountain peak to the south. It's the older Sister. The one to the west is the middle Sister, and the one to the north is the younger Sister. Anyway, I'm at Pine Ridge Ski Resort up on the older Sister. Head chef, temporarily sidelined to paperwork. Which is driving me crazy, making me grumpy, probably responsible for raising my blood pressure."

"So besides the obvious, let me guess. When you're at a desk, you're not exercising, and probably eating away your frustration? And getting angry thinking about what you'd rather be doing?"

Angela laughed. "Something like that. And I should know better, being a chef and a dietician, but I've been having a craving for salty things lately."

"Well, elevated blood pressure isn't necessarily a problem

when it's still in the high normal range the way yours is, so don't stress over that. But like I said, I want to keep an eye on it and make sure it isn't about something other than your change in lifestyle and…" Gabby smiled, thinking about the chocolate craving she'd been having for a while "…bad habits. So, for the next few days I'd like to see you every day to get a reading. Oh, and get back to the kitchen, at least on a part-time basis. Cook a little and use common sense." She scribbled a hasty note on her prescription pad. "According to your chart you're perfectly healthy, and I think it's good to stay working as long as you can. Light duty, though. Maybe some baking. The note gives you permission to get back into the kitchen on a limited basis, and I trust you'll use good judgment in deciding whether or not you feel like it."

"Really?" She read the note twice, blinking her surprise both times. "You're going to let me go back to work?"

"In case you haven't noticed, I'm not particularly an advocate of inactivity during pregnancy. People treat pregnancy like it's an illness, but I prefer to treat it like a normal condition, one the body's prepared to deal with."

"But Doc Graham said…" She stopped, frowned, then smiled. "I can work a little?"

Gabby laughed. "There's old-school and new-school thinking here. My dad, also an obstetrician, was a brilliant doctor, but he was very old school. Like Doc Graham. He thought pregnancy was a time when a woman should rest, put her feet up, be pampered. I, on the other hand, believe in the benefits of working through a pregnancy, if a woman's physical condition allows it. And studies back that up. My dad and I used to argue over this all the time."

"And who won?"

"He did with his patients. I did with mine." And neither of them ever budged from their position. "So, in other words, be indulgent. Of course, you're the one who has to define what indulgent is, according to your condition. Now, how about I do the rest of your physical, then we'll talk about the really important things, like decorating baby's room."

"So tell me about your hospital." Gabby caught up to Neil in the hall and fell into step with him. Big steps, tall man. Broad shoulders that swayed naturally with his steps. Neil Ranard had an impressive stature, and for Gabby to notice was something out of the ordinary. Usually she didn't pay attention, because most men looked her directly in the eyes, and she had a definite preference for tall. But he was tall, taller than Gabby by a good head, which put him well over six feet. Nice, considering how her five-feet-eight height towered over so many people. And intimidated so many men. "Tell me the five most important things I need to know in order to succeed here."

"Well, the first is that coffee breaks are essential. Do you prefer your coffee with, or without, cream and sugar?"

"We're on our way to a coffee break? That's why you're in such a big hurry?"

"Believe me, at the end of ski season, you look for any excuse you can find to take a break. For five months we're ridiculously busy. There's hardly enough time to catch your breath. Never enough time to sit down and put your feet up. Sometimes you're on call for days. Meaning, no coffee breaks whatsoever. Then the season changes and there's time to take a break, so you do even if you don't necessarily want one, because you know that will change in due course and soon you'll bemoan the fact that you don't have time to take a break. The two phases of our medical life here—with, and without, coffee breaks—are a vicious cycle."

"And you like that, don't you? I see it in your eyes."

Neil laughed. "Or maybe I just like to complain."

"Ah, the foibles of being self-indulgent. I just had a talk with my patient about that."

"My foibles have more to do with leaving here and being so damned grateful to come back, under *any* circumstance, break or no break. I was away for a while, working in a clinic in Los Angeles, somehow deluding myself into thinking that I wanted steady hours, five days a week. It was a job most doctors would envy, because I was able to live like everybody else does. You know, getting up in the morning, going to work, coming home in the evening. Weekends for tennis and golfing, which I absolutely hate, but did anyway because I had the time. It was so amazingly normal it drove me crazy inside four months. Probably because it wasn't…enough. Wasn't personal the way it is here in White Elk, and by the time I'd worked to the end of my contract, I was more than ready to come back here, where nothing is normal. For me, that makes it better." He motioned Gabby around the corner to the staff lounge, where he practically lunged at the coffee pot. "How do you take yours? I mean, I'm assuming you still allow yourself a little caffeine at this stage of your pregnancy."

"Caffeine in moderation is fine, and there's always decaffeinated coffee if the caffeine causes side effects. But I don't like coffee." She turned up her nose. "Used to, but after I got pregnant I lost my taste for it. Started craving hot chocolate."

"But you do like the coffee breaks, don't you?"

"As long as I can sit down and put my feet up then, yes, I like the coffee breaks." Which is exactly what she did. She sat down in one chair, then Neil nudged another one across the room to her, so she could prop up her feet.

"Is this your first?" he asked, sitting down next to her.

"Yes. And just so we can get past this awkward moment, I'm not married, don't plan to be married, I'm not involved in any kind of relationship with the baby's father or anyone else, and I'm very much looking forward to single mother-hood. And in case that sounds defensive, I really don't mean for it to be, but I've said this by rote a few dozen times and that's just the way it comes out now." So, if that wasn't an ice-breaker, nothing was. "And it's not a secret, Neil. People will ask, they'll want to talk, and that's fine. If I'm going to be here for a couple of months, I'd rather everyone knows this isn't one of those circumstances where they need to whisper and speculate. My pregnancy is the best thing that ever happened to me, and I'm ecstatic."

"I'm glad. When I was in family practice in Los Angeles, I saw too many pregnant patients who weren't ecstatic, and it made me...sad. Sad for the mother, sad for the baby." A deep frown confirmed his sentiment, but he wiped it away after a sip of coffee, and his normal sunny smile returned. "So, you asked me about the hospital, didn't you? Five important things everyone needs to know... Well, as you've seen, it's small. That's important because we like the intimacy. We have forty beds that can expand to fifty, if we have to. Sixty in a dire emergency. Also, we offer general service here, no elective major surgeries, emergency major surgery only when it's vital, and most minor procedures are welcomed. We special-ize in pediatrics, not so much because that's what we set out to do but by virtue of the fact that the two co-owners have pe-diatric specialties in their backgrounds, meaning we do get a few more peds referrals than we normally would. Although it's not technically a pediatric hospital." He paused, then grinned. "Was that four or five things?"

"Technically, four. So, you were in pediatrics?"

"Still am, but for White Elk and the whole Three Sisters area, it's too limiting, so I have a secondary specialty in family practice. Like my partner, Eric Ramsey. He was a pediatric surgeon, but to be flexible enough to work here he had to expand his horizons. So, besides a couple of doctors who seem to be the proverbial jacks-of-all-trades, we also have a state-of-the-art trauma department, headed by Eric, a full obstetrics department headed by, well, you, for the moment, a neonatal nursery, a good orthopedic set-up, and we also coordinate mountain rescue from here. Just a couple of ticks off full service on a very small scale—and growing, I guess you'd say. And now that's more than five."

"And I'm more than impressed. So, you're a co-owner?"

He nodded. "The hospital was struggling when I came back, and Eric Ramsey and I bought it in order to keep it going. In an area such as this you can't afford to have the hospital go under, because that affects the whole local economy. A ski resort area—and we have three ski resorts in the vicinity—needs a hospital nearby. So Eric and I decided to invest, and see if, together, we could get it back on track. So far, so good, if you don't count the fact that everybody here is grossly overworked and underpaid." He chuckled. "I get credit for the good stuff and I let Eric take credit for the bad. Although I think he says it the other way around. Anyway, you'll meet him when he gets over his sore throat…caught it from his twins. He's the one who coordinates mountain rescue, by the way."

"How many more doctors do you have?"

"Two full-time orthopedists, Kent Stafford and Jane McGinnis, John Ellis, who's another family practitioner, only he's part-time, in semi-retirement now, and we have a part-time rehabilitation specialist, Jackie Pennington, who comes in from Salt Lake city two days a week. Oh, and an obstetrician on the way, but not for another few weeks. We have nurse practitioner Fallon O'Gara, whom you met earlier and who practically runs the hospital—she's probably the most essential team member we have. And we have a couple of respiratory therapists, three physical therapists, and a dozen staff nurses. We also have a few doctors who come in to help out in the clinic on a rotating basis once or twice a month—a cardiologist and a rheumatologist. Then there's Henry Gunther, a retired anesthesiologist, on call. He moved here to engineer the ski train—trains were his hobby—so he's always close by when we need him. Then we have a number of volunteers and support staff, and that's about it. White Elk Hospital. Struggling, but surviving."

"Seems adequate for the area." And impressive. White Elk Hospital appeared to be a well-run medical facility, even if Neil did admit to a few shortcomings, and it was almost too bad she wouldn't be part of it for long. It could have been what she was looking for, professionally, anyway. Someplace nice, where people cared about each other

"Most of the time it is. And the one thing I failed to mention is that we all take our turns in the emergency department and trauma, even if that's not our specialty. At present, we don't have enough funds to staff it regularly, so we all get our chance to work there. I'm hoping that before the start of next year's skiing I'll be able to hire one more physician, another trauma doc, and bring in a couple of moonlighters. But Eric and I are still talking it over, crunching numbers, crossing our fingers."

"It sounds…compact." And not at all complicated, like so many of the large hospitals were—hospitals where the doctors fit into their own little niche and rarely, if ever, wandered out of it. Some might say there were advantages to staying where you belonged, but she liked the idea of working different areas, especially if the doctors' medical qualifications suited that. Her own father, an obstetrician, had been a general field surgeon in the army and she'd had training in general surgery, too, at his urging.

"Coming from Chicago, the way you do, I suppose it would."

"Well, coming from Chicago, the way I do, I have a different appreciation for what medicine should be."

"Which is?"

"Uncomplicated."

"In an ideal world," Neil said.

"In a real world, if that's how you want it to be. Where I worked, everything was complicated. The more complicated it became, the further away the patients seemed to get. I got used to it, I suppose, but..." She frowned. Shrugged. "It was OK then, but not any more."

"What changed you?"

"I'd like to attribute it to my pregnancy hormones but, to be honest, I haven't been happy for a while. Not unhappy either. Just existing. Nothing was wrong, nothing was bad. But nothing made me happy about my work, and I think to be a good doctor...to be the best doctor you can be...you need to be happy about your work. My dad always was. He jumped out of bed in the morning and couldn't wait to get started. He thrived in the complicated system, turned it into his playground and worked it to the advantage of his patients. I suppose I thought I should, too, which is why I stayed in practice with him so long, doing just that. But..." She shrugged again. "I wasn't suited to the manipulations, I guess you could say. I became too restless to be as effective as I wanted to be and decided I finally needed to make a change. Getting pregnant was the last shove I needed. Don't know what that permanent change is yet, but I'll know it when I see it." She was positive of that.

"So you came here, to White Elk, looking for...happiness?"

Not even close, but that was a complication she felt no pressing urge to discuss with him. "Handmade baby clothes and peace of mind. And I've already found the handmade baby clothes."

* * *

"I'm done for the day," Gabby said, plopping down onto the exam table in emergency room one. In the past two hours she'd seen one scheduled patient, one walk-in and done a regular pelvic exam on one of the staff nurses. It wasn't an overwhelming schedule, which was fine with her. Working again felt good. She'd missed it, and she was glad to be back in any capacity.

Neil, who was sitting on a chrome stool across from her, looking all rigid and uncomfortable whilst reading an outdated medical journal, glanced up, took off his reading glasses and tucked them into his pocket. "Did you have a good first day? It wasn't too much for you, was it?"

"Good first day, yes. Too much, no. In fact, it was a little slow."

"Like I said earlier, you'll learn to appreciate those lulls since they don't come too often." He put his journal aside, and stood up. "Look, are you up to a quick dinner? We're not busy right now. Fallon is down the hall stitching up a kid who took a header off his bicycle, and that's all we've had this past hour. So I was thinking about going across the street to the café before I have to come back and spend the night in emergency on call. You're welcome to join me, unless you have other plans."

"Plans? My plan this time yesterday was to go back to Chicago and get my condo ready to sell. Now here I am, working in a place I'd never heard of until…" she glanced at her watch "…twenty-nine hours, forty-two minutes ago. Meaning no plans, and I've love to join you."

"So, what do you eat?"

"Lately, everything I can get my hands on. A little light on meat, but other than that no dietary restrictions, no self-imposed taboos. Just point me in the direction of food and I'll show you what I eat."

"Then you'll love Catie's Overlook, because they fix a

little bit of everything." Neil hurried down to exam three to check on Fallon, who was coming along nicely with her patient. In fact, the procedure was finished and she was at the lollipop stage—the hardest part of the ordeal, trying to get her young patient to choose between red and green. Neil took a look at the stitches, wrote an antibiotic prescription, gave the boy both the red and the green, and sent him home with his mother. Then off with his white lab coat and on with his denim jacket. A quick gesture to Gabby and they were on their way.

"So what's the specialty of the house?" she asked. Heading down the hall, his strides were long, and his heels clicked briskly on tile floor. She liked that confidence in him, liked the way he held the door open for her but didn't overstep his bounds by taking hold of her arm as she half expected him to do. "And are the portions huge? Because I eat a lot these days. I tell myself it's because Bryce is going to be an athlete and he's storing up the calories early."

"Bryce?"

"My son. I'm calling him Bryce Evans, after my father." She sighed wistfully. "That was the first decision I made after I found out I was having a boy. A fitting tribute, I think."

"I take it your father's not with you any more?"

Not her father, not Bryce's father. Things should have been different. "Not any more. Just when I was ready to make the big move, he made a bigger one. Too young, too soon."

"I'm sorry, Gabrielle. I get the feeling you and your father were close."

"We were." Stepping up onto the curb, she stopped for a moment as Bryce kicked, and laid a hand on her belly. Then she smiled. "But it's an amazing circle of life, isn't it? I lose one Bryce who meant the world to me, and another one's about to enter my life who means even more."

* * *

What an amazing woman. He didn't think he'd ever met anyone like Gabrielle Evans before. Confident, self-assured. Maybe a little too defiant with her self-reliance, probably a reaction to her having a baby alone. He guessed that she probably fought against things she didn't have to, but that was OK. It made her even more interesting. So why was it that he'd met her now, when the timing was so wrong on so many different levels? "Table for two, Helen," he said to the waitress who greeted them at the door. "Oh, and this is Dr Evans. She'll be working as our obstetrician for the next few weeks."

Helen looked down at the lump under Gabby's coat with a dubious frown, then nodded. "Which Sister?" she asked. Catie's Overlook boasted the best view in town—windows overlooking each of the Three Sisters.

"Older Sister. Better view, more lights." Not that it really mattered, since he'd seen each of the Sisters from every angle more times than he could remember, but he thought Gabrielle might like the nicer view.

"Angela Blanchard works up there," Gabby commented as Neil pulled out the chair for her.

It was quaint, old-fashioned, all wood, and surprisingly not as uncomfortable as it looked. But on the other side of the room there were cozy, romantic booths, where several couples sat all tucked into each other. He'd done that, once upon a time. In fact, he'd brought Karen here, and he'd been the one so distracted by the moment that he hadn't noticed the obvious—that she had eyes for him, but not him alone. Well, not any more. He'd sworn off relationships a while ago, and he wasn't yet in the mood to swear back on. If he ever did, there would be no cozy booths and candlelight, though. Next time, it was going to be a matter of practicality. His one and only promise to himself was head before heart. A down-to-earth partnership.

"She came into the clinic today," Gabby continued.

"Grumpy?" Neil asked, as he took his seat, purposely keeping his back toward the row of romantic booths. "She usually is lately."

"No, not grumpy. More like frustrated with her situation. And with her inactivity. So I gave her permission to return to work, be active again on a limited basis, which is what she wanted. It had a pretty good effect on her mood."

"Ah, going against Walt Graham's sage advice to stay home and keep your feet up for nine months. His wife had seven children, and we always teased that she kept getting pregnant so she could take the nine-month holiday. Because Walt wouldn't let her do a thing. He waited on her hand and foot, and hired someone to do it for him when he wasn't there."

"And…"

"He was lost after she died. Lost a lot of the joy in his life, I think. Woke up one morning a few weeks ago and said it was time to do something else, and he did. He quit his practice. Now he's out hiking in the woods, skiing, doing the things he never had time to do before. But he's a good man, and a good doctor with old-fashioned ways."

"He sounds a lot like my father. Dad always had my mother on a pedestal. It's hard for me to even imagine the kind of love he had for her, but I think that's what Walt Graham must have had for his wife, because Dad never got over her after she died. Never dated, never looked at another woman, never took off his wedding ring."

"How old were you when she died?"

"Six. It was tough for him, raising me alone, because I was rambunctious. I demanded a lot of attention from him for the first few years, and the less time he had to give me, the more I demanded. At least that's the way it was when I was young. It got better…for me. Which made it better for my dad. But sometimes I wonder how tough it's going to be for me raising a child by myself, because I remember the nights my dad would shut himself in his room. I used to think I could hear him crying…and I believed it was my fault that he was sad. I think, though, that he was overwhelmed. He would always tell me that a child needed two parents, and he was sorry I had only one."

"He sounds amazing."

"He was. I spent a lot of time at his side, being his little assistant, walking along with him carrying his medical bag, pretending to be a doctor, too. It wasn't the way most of my friends were growing up, but I never really missed out on anything, because I loved my life, loved it that my dad included me in his medical life whenever he could. It made me feel special…important." She blinked hard, fighting back fat tears welling in her eyes. "Anyway, I know Walt Graham had his ways, but I have mine, and I don't think there's a need to keep healthy pregnant women from working, as long as they want to work, and they're physically able."

"Are we talking about Angela Blanchard, or you?"

"Both. I want her to work because she wants to work. And I want to work in the emergency room like everybody else does when it's their turn. But I got the impression that you might not want me there. If that's because you don't know me, I totally understand. But if it's because I'm pregnant…"

"I do know you. At least what I can know from a background check. You come with glowing references, Gabrielle. The kind that would make me want to put you on the emergency schedule if I had room. But I'm scheduled two weeks out, and unless there's an emergency, I usually don't change the schedule. That's why you're not there right now. The only reason. Because I am a full-fledged supporter of women, pregnant or not, doing what they want to do. Maybe we got off on the wrong foot when I told you to go put your feet up and rest, and when I tried showing you back to the lodge, but that was just me, doing a poor job of being a gentleman to a pregnant woman who seemed to be lost."

"I wasn't lost. In fact, I was on my way in when you came outside. And you're not that bad at being a gentleman," she teased. "Maybe a little more old-fashioned than you think you are, but it's nice."

Not to hear Karen talk about it. His ex-wife had accused him of so many things over the course of their marital break-up, and he was pretty sure his skills at being a gentleman had probably fallen in there somewhere. "Let's just say that I'm out of practice, and for the foreseeable future I don't expect to be getting much practice." Work was easier. It didn't betray him the way his wife had.

"This is the part where I *don't* ask questions, right? Because I've never been very good at the distinctions. Some people say something leading, like you did, then drop it, hoping to really drop it. Others say something leading, then drop it, hoping the other person will pick it up. But I'm sensing that you don't want me to do that…to pick it up and ask questions."

"Failed marriage. In and out quickly with a lot of ugliness in the middle. That's about all there is to say about it."

"Even though I've never been married, I know that's *never* all there is to say about it, Neil, but I won't ask."

She really did fascinate him. There were so many complex layers to her, it could take a lifetime to peel them all back to reveal the full essence of Gabrielle Evans. What an astonishing lifetime that could be for some lucky man. "Are you always so direct?" he asked.

She nodded. "I attribute it to my relationship with my dad. He was a busy man, didn't have time to waste, and he'd always tell me that if I wanted to know, ask. If I wanted to be heard, speak up. Worked for him, works for me."

"Your dad was right, and being direct is oddly becoming on you."

She wrinkled her nose, forcing back an almost shy smile.

"You don't take compliments very well, do you?"

"In my experience, compliments often come with conditions. So let's just say that the one offering the compliment has to grow on me before I'm comfortable with the compliments."

"Am I growing on you yet?"

"Sprouting," she said.

Yes, she was very direct, and he liked it more and more. In fact, he seriously doubted that Gabrielle could ever lie, or be even the slightest bit deceitful. So where had *she* been when he'd been convincing himself he loved Karen? Because Gabrielle Evans, in the right place at the right time, could have changed so many things in his life.

CHAPTER THREE

"I THOUGHT you'd gone home after our meal." Neil picked up the last of the gauze scraps and tossed them in the trash, then snapped off his gloves and dropped them in the trash, too.

"I did, actually. Got ready for bed. Lay down. Couldn't sleep. Decided to take a walk, and here I am."

"Let me guess. You were the top student in your medical-school class."

"Why would you say that?"

"Because you couldn't do anything less. You're the obsessed type who never eases down, and being anything but the top student would have driven you crazy."

"Is that a bad thing?"

Neil laughed. "For most people, probably. For you, it's kind of cute. So, did you try counting sheep?"

"Did that. Got to about a million, then tried reading a medical journal. That didn't work either, so I took a walk, only it stimulated me even more."

"So you want me to do what? Bore you to sleep?"

"For me, boredom means an empty mind. An empty mind means more time to think. More thinking means less sleep."

"In other words, you came here to work."

"I saw several patients in the waiting area. You could use me, couldn't you? Since you're the only one on."

"Nobody ever wins with you, do they, Gabrielle?"

"I try not letting it happen too often."

"And I'm not getting rid of you, am I?"

She shook her head.

"Room three. Mrs Blondell. Indigestion. She probably had oysters for dinner."

"That's it? All I get is indigestion?"

"Take it or leave it, Doctor." He grinned. "Sometimes I get to win, too."

On her way to exam three, Gabby thought about how much she liked Neil. He was just…easy. Easy to talk to, easy to be around. "So, what can I do for you this evening, Mrs Blondell?"

In response, the round, ruddy woman burped. Then giggled. Then burped again. "Oysters," she said. "Happens every time I eat them."

"Have you ever thought about not eating them?"

"I limit myself to once a month." Rumbling burp. "And the consequences are annoying, but worth it."

"Then how about taking some kind of a preventative before you indulge so that you can cut down on the consequences?"

"A month's worth of preventative for one night of indulgence? That's a high price to pay for an occasional weakness, don't you think?" Mrs Blondell held her breath while Gabby listened to her chest, then her belly.

When she was finished, satisfied that nothing but a good case of acid indigestion was going on, Gabby pulled the stethoscope from her ears and took her patient's pulse. "In my experience, you're going to pay one way or another. Trust me, the cure won't be so bad, and you'll be able to have oysters twice a month, if that's what you want."

"Was it oysters?" Neil asked a little while later as they passed in the hall.

"I gave her a few antacid samples to take home with her, and prescribed an antacid to take on a regular basis."

"Which she won't take. Won't even buy. In fact, you'll find your prescription torn up and tossed in the trash on the way out."

"So why does she bother coming in?"

"Lonely. She's seventy-two, widowed, and I think some of her evenings get pretty long. She eats oysters to remind her of her husband, even though they don't agree with her any more. They went out on the twenty-eighth of every month for fifty years and celebrated their marriage with a romantic dinner."

"And had oysters," Gabby said, as a gush of weepy hormonal tears overtook her. "And today's the twenty-eighth. That's so sweet." She brushed at the unexpected tears with her hand, but Neil fished a clean tissue from his pocket and handed it to her.

"What's sweet is fifty years with the same person," he said, his voice a little thin. "More like a miracle."

"Spoken like a man who's jaded about marriage." Sniffles coming to an end, she stepped over to the nearest sink and washed her hands.

"Jaded about one marriage in particular. Admiring of the ones that make it." He gave her a patient chart. "Room five, mysterious rash. Nothing sentimental as far as I can tell."

"Well, one bad marriage doesn't a bad institution make. In my opinion."

"Eternal optimist?"

"Don't you have to be when you're a doctor? Especially an obstetrician?" She took the chart from him. "Or even someone falling in love?" Without awaiting an answer, Gabby

marched straight into a full hour of incidental complaints—
nothing too taxing, nothing communicable. Because Neil was
considerate. He could have stuck her with the flu patient who
came in dehydrated and coughing, or the man with the gashed
hand who was loud and obnoxious, but he didn't. He was protecting her. Giving her what she wanted by allowing her to
work yet looking out for her at the same time.

If they'd been more than colleagues, she might have considered that a little romantic. Maybe not as much as oysters,
but nice all the same.

So why wasn't a man like Neil Ranard taken? He was a
looker in every way that should attract a woman. Great per-
sonality. Considerate. Good doctor. Yet he seemed to have no
life outside his work. It didn't seem like he wanted one. So,
why was that?

It did make her wonder, especially when she stood off to
the side in the emergency department, as she was doing now,
watching him work, watching him interact with other people.
He was with a grumpy child. A *loud*, grumpy child with a tummy ache. The little boy had been crying for fifteen minutes,
then Neil pulled back the curtain, entered the emergency
cubicle, and…what was that he did? Did Neil make a funny
face? She couldn't tell, but suddenly the child was laughing.
No words even spoken.

The way he related to his patients was simply astonishing.
And the way they responded to him… Just like the little boy did.
People lit up around him. Reacted in amazing ways. Come to
think of it, she had reacted like everybody else did.

Well, one thing was certain. Whatever kept Neil estranged
in his personal life had to be his choice. Because as she
watched him work, she noticed any number of admirers who
would have loved being included in his off-duty hours. The
clerk at the emergency desk who couldn't keep her eyes off

Neil, the volunteer who giggled when he got near her, the grumpy little boy's mother... Neil Ranard had a way about him when he was being a doctor. Just not so much in the personal sense. "So, anything else?" Gabby asked when he left the child's cubicle. She was actually beginning to feel a little tired. "Because I think now would be a good time for me to go back to the cabin and get some rest. Unless you need me."

Rather than looking at her, he looked straight at her belly. "Your baby is the one who needs you right now...needs you to be rested." Then he looked at her. Stared straight into her eyes, with no attempt to rush the encounter—apparently lost in thought before he finally spoke. "So, go. Take care of yourself. And Bryce."

It surprised her to hear him say her baby's name. Until now, no one ever had. They always said *the baby* or *it*. But, honestly, she was pleased that he'd even remembered Bryce's name, and hearing it from someone else gave her an unexpected thrill, like she wasn't the only one in the world who thought of her child as a real person. "For once, I'm not going to argue." She arched her back, then raised her hand to rub the small of it, but Neil stepped behind her and started a gentle massage to her shoulders.

"You don't mind me doing this, do you? Chivalry may be a little old-fashioned, but sometimes old-fashioned is called for."

Rather than answering, she responded with a groan that sounded more like a purr. And did it again when he found a particularly tight muscle in her neck. "Magic hands," she murmured, not intending to say it out loud.

"In that case, gratuities accepted."

His hands moved back to her shoulders and it was all Gabby could do to keep herself from going weak in the knees and collapsing right into his arms. "And what kind of gratuity would you like, Dr Ranard?"

"Haven't decided. But I'll let you know when I think of it."

"Sounds fair. But I reserve the right to make conditions."

"I figured you would. In fact, being direct the way you are, I never thought you would have it any other way."

Gabby started to laugh, but at that moment Neil discovered a very sore spot between her shoulder blades, and what started as a laugh turned into a groan. "You know you could make money with those hands," she said, her voice a little raspy. "Open a massage therapy clinic…"

"You'd be my first patient?"

His hands splayed out from shoulder to shoulder, and his fingers applied that perfect amount of pressure—pressure that verged on both pain and pleasure at the same time. The hurt that felt so good. It wouldn't take much for her to become addicted to this…on a regular basis. "First in line." Whole body treatment. His hands everywhere… Well, that was a thought a woman in her advanced condition shouldn't be having. But she couldn't help it. If the rest was as good as this…

"I heard you and Neil had dinner together last night." Laura Stewart sat down across from Gabby and plunked her coffee mug on the table, indicating she was going to stay awhile.

"Small-town talk," Gabby replied. She'd slept in late since she had no early morning appointments, had a leisurely breakfast, and was now enjoying a lazy view of the main street, watching all the people heading off to their various destinations. Some were in a hurry, some were not. Some drove cars, others walked, a few ran. And there were a handful of brave souls on bicycles, pedaling against the chilly air, which gave Gabby the shivers, even sitting so close to the lodge's large stone fireplace, with its morning fire all crackling and cozy.

What she could see from her favorite table was an amazing snapshot of everyday life, but there was so much space in

White Elk. Nothing was crammed in here. Not the buildings, not the people. And the street was not permeated with the sounds of impatient motorists honking, and passers-by shouting their anger and frustrations for anyone to hear, like she'd grown accustomed to in Chicago.

Gabby felt good here. Maybe that was what she liked best about this little town. She didn't fit in, didn't know anybody. Didn't even have any kind of a life here. But she felt good, maybe even more optimistic about her future than she had for quite a while. Truth was, she didn't especially mind the small-town talk, even when it involved her.

"Then it's true? You did?"

Gabby shrugged. "I had dinner, he had dinner. And, coincidentally, we sat at the same table. So I guess the answer is yes, but not to the things people might imply from it."

"Ah, but rumors still fly, no matter how you might want to defend yourself. And up here, at this elevation, where the air is clearer, they seem to fly a little faster."

"You mean the rumor about the pregnant stranger and the handsome town doctor?" She laughed. "It may sound like the title of a romance novel, but I'm afraid it was just dinner. He ate. I ate, and ate, and ate…"

"We worry about Neil because he doesn't take time for himself. Doesn't have a lot of fun in life. And I'm not going to spread rumors here, or tell you anything I shouldn't, but everybody I know wants him to have…more. Good things. Happiness. He deserves it."

Laura sipped her coffee while Gabby pondered what she'd just said. So Neil was a bit of a recluse? Or maybe so dedicated to his work that he got lost in it? Honestly, she could relate to that. Her father had been much the same way, and to a great extent she took after her father in that. Her dad had buried himself in work because he'd lost the love of his life much too early. And she'd buried herself because that's all she'd known. Maybe for Neil it wasn't a bad thing, being that way. According to Laura, though, it wasn't such a good thing either. "Well, when the rumor flies your way again, would you mind infusing it with a bit of truth, that it was a casual dinner between two medical colleagues? That's all. No need for speculations."

"I think there might be some disappointment with that," Laura replied.

"Haven't people noticed the obvious about me?"

"People notice what they want to notice. Carol Vincent, the night clerk at the hospital, said Neil looked happy when he came back from dinner. Apparently that was much more obvious to her than your condition."

"And?"

"We don't see that smile on him much. That's what made it so noticeable."

"So when he does smile, it starts a rumor?"

Laura laughed. "Under normal circumstances, I'd say no. But because it's Neil, and because he's so well loved… Look, I've got to get busy. I just wanted to stop by for a moment, say hello, see if there's anything you need."

Anything she needed? Now, that was a loaded question because the honest truth was, she did need, but she wasn't sure what. "I'm fine," she said, trying to figure out what should be on the top of her list of needs. "A little surprised that I'll be staying here for a while… You don't mind me staying in the cabin, do you?"

"I love having you in the cabin. Normally at this time of the year there's no one to talk to, so this is good. And I know Angela is glad you're here. With what she's been going through lately…" Laura stopped abruptly.

"What?" Gabby asked.

"If I told you, that would be small-town gossip, wouldn't it?" Laughing, Laura scooted away from the table. "Anyway, I just wanted to let you know that it's good to have you here, and I'm hoping that after six weeks you'll decide to call it home."

A lot could happen in six weeks, but for now Gabby decided that no decision was the best one. Liking the texture of the little town was one thing, but settling down here and setting up a new life…she just didn't know if that's what she really wanted to do. Of course, she didn't know if that was *not* what she wanted to do either.

After Laura scurried off to do whatever it was she had to do, Gabby bundled up for her walk to the hospital. Her morning schedule was light, but she did have patients to see. And according to her schedule, the day was going to begin with some kind of a dedication. She wasn't sure what, wasn't even sure she was going to go see what it was about. But when she arrived at the hospital, the entry corridor was bustling with people. Dozens of them, all headed in the same direction.

"What's this about?" she asked Fallon O'Gara.

"The hospital staff voted to name the newly remodeled pediatrics ward after Neil's brother. He endowed it with sufficient funds for a nice expansion, and we're having the dedication ceremony this morning." She glanced at her watch. "In five minutes, actually. Guess I'd better hurry. I'm the one who's supposed to meet the mayor and escort her to the podium."

A dedication, the mayor… This was a big event, apparently as much for the town as it was for the hospital. To be honest, Gabby was a little curious to meet Neil's brother. In fact, until this very moment she hadn't even known he had a brother. Not that it really mattered since she knew nothing at all about Neil. But the buzz of excitement was a little contagious, as more and more people hurried down one of the halls she'd yet to explore. So, why not? She was a part of this, if only for a while. And she didn't have a patient scheduled in for half an hour.

Gabby blended into one of the waves of people sloshing its way toward a central corridor outside Pediatrics, but when she got there, she was shocked to see at least three-hundred people packed in, shoulder to shoulder. "Come up front with the staff," Fallon called to her. "We're going to have photos taken."

Neil was standing front and center when she reached the front of the room, looking very uncomfortable about the whole thing. People were mingling, smiling, laughing and he was standing alone, not talking, not smiling, definitely not mingling.

"You don't like these kinds of things?" she asked him, feeling as out of place here as he looked.

"It was a nice gesture, donating the money, but there's no need for all the fuss. Just hang the damned plaque and be done with it."

Not only did he look uncomfortable, he was downright grumpy. And it wasn't about the plaque, she guessed. She wanted to ask, or at least inquire which face in the crowd belonged to Neil's brother, but the mayor superseded her by stepping up to the microphone and thanking the crowd for coming. "As you are all aware, a generous endowment has been given to this hospital, for the purpose of establishing a state-of-the-art pediatrics ward."

The crowd applauded, and Neil looked even more agitated.

"It is with great regret that our generous benefactor is no longer with us…"

As in dead? Gabby wondered. Or maybe he didn't live in White Elk now. A quick look at Neil's face didn't reveal the answer. In fact, as the mayor droned on for another few minutes, the tight expression on Neil's face stayed fixed. She wasn't even sure he blinked.

"And with no further ado, I'd like to ask Neil to unveil the plaque."

The audience applauded again, but Neil didn't budge.

"Neil?" the mayor prodded.

In response he gave a curt nod of his head, then walked, with all the stiffness of a robot, across the tile floor to the wall with the still-draped plaque on it. And just as stiffly, he reached up and pulled the drape away, letting the burgundy fabric slip straight through his fingers to the floor.

People applauded as the bronze letters set into marble were revealed, and it took Gabby's eyes a few moments to shift from Neil's face to the plaque, where the words *The Gavin Thierry Pediatrics Ward* simply didn't sink in at first. So she blinked twice, looked again, gasped for breath, and stumbled backwards...her head spinning, her immediate world growing dim...dimmer...

The last thing she heard was the collective gasp from the crowd as she pitched backwards.

CHAPTER FOUR

"GABRIELLE?"

The voice sounded distant, but she knew it wasn't.

"Gabrielle, can you hear me?"

There was light shining in her eyes. Bright light. She could feel the intensity of it even though her eyes were shut.

"Come on, Gabrielle. Look at me."

Someone was holding her hand, too. It was Neil. Even without looking, she knew that. Knew the tingle he caused…

"Open your eyes, Gabrielle."

She wanted to, but there was something she didn't want to see. Something she couldn't quite remember.

"How's her blood pressure?"

Now, that was a voice she didn't remember. Nice, deep, rich. Not as nice as Neil's voice, though.

"A little high. Not enough to cause her to faint."

Ah, Neil's voice. The nicest voice she'd ever heard.

"Well, the fetal heartbeat is strong. Nothing going wrong there, as far as I can tell."

The other voice again. Nice enough voice, but Neil's was better. More soothing.

"It's a good thing I caught her. She could have hurt herself on the marble floor," Neil said.

Yes, Neil's voice was the nicest. It made her feel…safe.

"Blood sugar's normal. Oh, and, Neil, I'm having the lab run a full blood panel."

"Thanks, Eric."

"Has she mentioned any kind of past medical history? Or has she been exhausted?" Eric Ramsey asked, looking down at Gabrielle. "She's not particularly pale, not underweight."

"She eats a lot. Fallon did a physical on her, and nothing came to light. Gabrielle's a really staunch defender of women working through their pregnancy if they feel well enough to do it, but now I'm wondering if she has some underlying condition she doesn't know about. Or something developing…"

Eric scratched his head. "Well, whatever it is, she sure picked a dramatic moment to faint."

"I didn't faint," she finally said. "I just…just had a momentary syncope."

"Isn't that the same as fainting?" Neil asked.

His wasn't the face directly over her when she did manage to open her eyes. In fact, when her blur came into focus she was greeted by a startling, handsome set of clear green eyes. Chestnut-colored hair, cut short. Angular face. A breath-taker for sure, but not her type. "We haven't really been formally introduced, have we?" she asked, extending her hand upward to Eric.

Quite surprised by the gesture, he took it. "I don't suppose we have."

"And these aren't the best circumstances for a proper introduction, but I'm Gabby Evans."

"Eric Ramsey," he replied, looking over at Neil, who

looked almost like he was ready to pass out too. "And what I want to know from you, Gabby Evans, is what happened?"

"Odd thing about fainting. Most of the time you don't really know what happened. One minute you're there, the next you're not." She started to sit up, but Neil stepped up to the exam table and placed a hand on her shoulder.

"There's always a cause, Gabrielle," Neil insisted.

There was. She knew that. But how could she tell Neil what that cause was?

"I think I spun around too quickly, got light-headed." Horrible lie. But it was the best she could do under the circumstances. "And I'm fine now. I heard you say that the fetal heartbeat is strong. That my blood sugar is normal. So, I'm ready to go." She tried sitting up again but, like the first time, Neil stopped her.

"You're going back to work, aren't you?" he asked.

"Is there any reason I shouldn't?"

"Other than you just fainted?" he snapped.

"Look, you two," Eric interjected. "I need to go see a patient of my own, plus I think I'll look in on the patient Gabby's had waiting for half an hour. Gabby, it's nice to finally meet you *officially*, and I'm glad you're feeling better. Neil, her blood work should be back shortly. If you need anything…" Eric slipped out of the exam room without another word, his absence barely even noticed by Gabby and Neil, who were staring at each other like two rancorous tomcats ready to have a go at each other.

"I'm fine," she insisted. Truth was, she wanted to get away from him. *Right now!* Wanted to think, to figure out how this could have happened. She was pregnant with Neil's brother's baby, of all the incredible coincidences. Incredible and, she had a feeling, not in a good way. "And I'll take it easy the rest of the day." Except her hands were shaking now, and she was so cold she was shivering. Shock, followed by a faint had a way of doing all that. And Neil wasn't missing a symptom, which meant he wasn't going to let her go anywhere. "Neil, I'm really fine," she managed, as another cold chill came over her. "I just got a little claustrophobic, started to panic, with all those people standing around. I'm not a great one for being in crowds. So I spun around, got light-headed, and…"

"And scared the hell out of me."

"Are you the one who caught me?"

"Caught you and carried you here."

"Then I'm sorry to have taken you away from the dedicatory ceremony. Were you supposed to make a speech?"

"I was glad for an excuse to get away from there, but not for the reason that made it happen." He picked up a blood-pressure cuff and wrapped it around Gabby's arm. Then he inflated the ball, put the stethoscope earpieces in his ears, and listened. Moments later, he pulled the earpieces out, and removed the cuff. "Normal." Then he glanced at the fetal monitor and nodded. "That's normal, too. So, do you want to tell me what this was really about?"

"I already told you, Neil. And when the rest of the lab results get back, you're not going to find anything wrong in them. I'm fine. I just had—"

"I know. A little syncope. And just so you won't go getting any crazy ideas that you'll rest for another hour, then go back to work, I've scheduled you out for the day. You're going back to the cabin and going straight to bed. Orders from your doctor, orders from your boss."

His tone made it clear he would take no argument. To be honest, though, she didn't want to argue. Didn't know what she wanted to do except get away from the hospital, away from Neil. "My patients… It's only my second day here, and I need to—"

"We're covered, Gabrielle. Eric and I can cover, so can John Ellis, another family practitioner. And Fallon's certainly capable of seeing patients if the need arises. So we're good here."

"Possibly half a day? I could go home for the rest of the morning and rest, then this afternoon…" She wasn't sure why she was arguing when she really did want to leave. Was it to impress Neil, show him that she could work, no matter what? Was it to prove the same to herself? She was afraid that he might decide to let her go altogether. Maybe he thought she was weak, she was a burden, he didn't need her. Horrible, horrible thought, since a little speck of optimism deep inside was telling her White Elk could be *the* place.

Neil shook his head adamantly at her suggestion. "You're not staying. And one of the good things about being the owner is that you get to boss people around." He smiled. "I kind of like it."

"Except you're not the bossy type." He didn't have a bossy bone in his body.

"Maybe not under ordinary circumstances, but this isn't an ordinary circumstance."

"Will you let me come back? When the blood tests reveal that nothing is wrong with me, and after I've spent the day resting, will you let me come back tomorrow?"

For a moment he looked surprised. Then his surprise was overcome by a generous smile. "I'm not going to fire you, Gabrielle. But I'm going to caution you the way you caution your patients, by telling you to use common sense. You, better than anybody else, know what you can do, and what you cannot do. And if that doesn't work, I have one magic word that will do it."

"What?"

"Bryce." He chuckled. "Was I right? Did that do it?"

"You were right. That did it," she conceded, not even resenting him for knowing how to get to her. Honestly, it was nice having someone care for her, and while Neil was only a casual acquaintance, he still did make her feel cared for. "Can I at least borrow some medical journals to take with me?"

"Wouldn't you rather be reading articles on how to decorate a baby's nursery?"

"Maybe I would, if the baby had a nursery. But he doesn't." And maybe he wouldn't here in White Elk after all. "So, the journals, please?"

"How about I bring them up to the cabin, along with some lunch and the results of your blood work in a couple of hours? You can rest until I get there, OK? Oh, and our security guard, Ed Lester, is waiting outside to drive you home right now, so you go on, and I'll be up in a while."

"You don't have to do that, Neil. I can take care of myself."

"Maybe I want to." His voice was tender, sincere.

A voice she could get used to.

As Neil helped Gabby first into a wheelchair, which, of course, she protested, then into Ed Lester's car, Gabby wondered why Neil was so willing to do so much for her, and she was still wondering the same thing five minutes later when Ed Lester stopped the car in front of the cabin, and helped her out. "Did you know Neil's brother very well?" she asked the gray-haired security guard, who had a firm hold on her as they walked up the cabin's wooden steps.

"Who, Gavin? We all knew him. Grew up right here in White Elk, practiced here until he and Neil…" He paused. Frowned. Didn't finish his sentence.

So Gabby asked, even though the way her heart was thudding told her the answer before Ed Lester could. "His name was Gavin? Gavin Thierry?" Even though she knew, she wanted to make sure.

The man nodded solemnly. "Damn shame what happened to him. He was a good doctor. Probably as good as his brother."

Gabby fought back a hard lump in her throat as she entered the cabin, and went straight to the rocking chair next to the fireplace. A fire would have been nice, but she lacked the physical energy to lay one. Lacked the emotional energy to do anything other than sit there and rock, and hope the numbing squeak of the rockers would keep everything else out of her mind. Because, right now, she truly didn't want to think.

But eventually confused thoughts started popping and, try as she may, she couldn't push them away. What had Ed Lester meant when he'd said Gavin had practiced here until he and Neil…? He and Neil what? Of all the times for the small-town gossip to quit on her! Especially when it concerned her, indirectly.

Which brought her to another weighty thought. Should she tell Neil about her involvement with his brother? She was, after all, carrying Gavin's son, Neil's nephew. "I don't know what to do, Bryce," she said on a heavy, discouraged sigh. "I was prepared to tell your father about you, but now that he's gone, I'm not sure what to do beyond that. Especially since…" Since what? Since she really liked Neil. Since she might be developing feelings for Neil, crazy as that seemed in two short days. "Like it would even go somewhere if I weren't pregnant," she muttered.

But she did wonder about her feelings. Naturally, she attributed them to her upsurge of hormones, and to a lesser extent the fact that she was alone and Neil was so…welcoming. So steady.

Leaning her head back against the rocker and shutting her eyes, the only thing Gabby envisioned was Neil, and in her images he was proving himself to be everything she'd ever wanted in a man. And that wasn't the hormones talking. Or the misfit wanderings of a delusional mind. "But I'm not going to fall in love, Bryce. We're fine, the two of us. No outsiders necessary. Right?"

What was she supposed to do, though, when that outsider was a blood relative to her baby? That was the question causing her hands to shake.

Slumping down into the rocker even more, Gabby sighed heavily again. Right about now she surely could have used some of her father's sage advice. There was never a time she could remember that he hadn't known what to do and say, and what had always amazed her about him had been how he'd utter just a few simple words that would make things crystal clear. She did miss him, and even now, after all these months without him, tears pooled in her eyes when thoughts of him flooded back. Daddy's girl—not because he was her only parent but because she wanted to be daddy's girl. His absence didn't change that, and the ache of missing him was an ache that was softened only by knowing that, in the coming years, there would be so many wonderful stories to tell Bryce about his grandfather.

Why couldn't life have been just a little less complicated right now?

"You know I haven't done this before," she said to Bryce, brushing away the tears with the back of her hand. "So you're going to have to bear with me until I get it right." And whether or not to tell Neil about his brother's baby was something she had to get right.

Gabby sat and rocked for the next hour, wrapped up in a cozy blanket and also wrapped in her memories of the past and her hopes for the future. She deliberately avoided thinking about Neil, pushing those thoughts right out when they crept in. After a while, when she'd finally succeeded in not thinking about him every three minutes, a sharp knock on her cabin door brought all thoughts of him right back to the forefront of her mind. He was here now, bringing lunch. She'd almost forgotten his offer. Wished she'd called and told him not to come.

But she hadn't, so she had to face him. "We're going to let the moment play itself out as it happens," she told Bryce on her way to the door. As she passed the hall mirror she took a quick glance, saw that she was a little more tear-splotched than she wanted him to see, so she pulled open the cabin door, then ran immediately to the sink in the bathroom to blot water on her face.

"You OK, Gabrielle?" Neil called from the hall.

"Fine," she called back, bent over the sink, cupping her hands under the water, then splashing it on her face. "Just washing my hands." And trying to wash away so many thoughts. Another quick look in the mirror convinced her to run a brush through her hair and tint her lips with a little colored gloss. Hasty, but not so revealing now, she decided as she turned out the bathroom light and emerged into the hall, where Neil stood waiting for her, much closer than she'd expected him to be.

"That was a long hand wash," he said, his face full of concern. "Unless you're scrubbing for surgery."

"I'm pregnant. I'm allowed to take longer doing things."

"Sure you're OK?"

She managed a smile, and a lie. "I'm OK." Which she wasn't. "And hungry." Which she was, but not nearly so much as usual. "So, let's eat." Skip the chat, go straight to the food and hope conversation between them could be cut to a minimum, because she didn't feel much like talking.

"Gabrielle, you look… Have you been crying?"

Neil reached out to take hold of her arm as she whisked by him, but as she slipped past, she grabbed the sack from his hands and hurried off toward the tiny cabin kitchen, anxious to get out of his gaze, lest he looked any deeper and discovered more. He was trying to diagnose her. She was sure of it, and if he thought he saw something, he wouldn't let her work, which would mean she had no reason to stay in White Elk. Leaving here might be the easiest solution, but it wasn't the one that felt good to her. And right now she truly needed to be back in the hospital, seeing patients and not being one. "Of course I wasn't crying. I just washed my face, got a little soap in my eyes. So, what did you hear back from the lab tests?"

"Everything's normal. Perfect."

She managed a wispy smile. "Just like I told you."

"You're right about that. You did tell me. But what you didn't tell me was why you fainted, and I think you know."

She glanced away from him, looked at the vegetable salad he'd brought for fear he could read the answer in her eyes. "You brought pastries, too?" she asked, pulling a cinnamon roll from the bag, breaking off a piece and immediately sticking it in her mouth so she wouldn't have to answer him.

"OK, I won't ask again. But if you faint again, Gabrielle, I won't be able to let you come back to work. In fact, I'll admit you to the hospital for the rest of your pregnancy. I don't like the way you're evading my question, but I'll respect your right to do it."

"I won't faint again," she said, once her mouth was empty.

"I hope not." He watched her go after another bite of cinnamon roll. "So, at least answer this question for me. Didn't anybody ever tell you that dessert comes *after* the meal?"

She licked the gooey icing off her fingers, then finally met him eye to eye. "My dad always told me to go after what I wanted and not to let anything get in my way, and right now I want the cinnamon roll." She picked up another cinnamon roll and handed it to him. "Care to join me and indulge yourself in the best part of the meal first?" Putting her already half-eaten roll on a plate, she went to the fridge to pour herself a glass of milk. One for her and, on impulse, one for Neil who, she noticed, looked awfully tempted to take a bite of his roll. Desire over tradition. Sometimes that was a nice dilemma to be caught in.

"And you don't think I might really want the salad first?"

She gave her head a vigorous shake no as she handed him his milk. "What I think is that you're in a rut. You think you're supposed to eat the salad first, and the cinnamon roll comes last because that's the traditional order of things, but that's only prior indoctrination. An old habit. If you really like the salad better than the cinnamon roll, then by all means, eat that first. But if you like the roll better, why fill up on the food that's not your preference and risk not having room left over for the food that is?"

It made sense to her, and she remembered the many meals when her father had let her start with the chocolate cake or the apple pie before she got to the meat and potatoes because of what she'd just said to Neil. Not every meal had been that way, of course. But her father always said that because life was so usual most of the time, why not be *unusual* when you had the chance? He'd always told her that it was healthy to be different, and she'd believed him. Still did.

Suddenly, her eyes brimmed once more with tears and she spun away before Neil could see them.

"I was right. You're crying," he said, setting down his glass of milk and stepping up behind her.

"You're not supposed to notice." Gabby sniffled. "I'm having a hormonal couple of hours. Nothing to worry about."

"Would another massage help?"

A massage would be heaven. Wouldn't do a thing for her hormones, and her muscles weren't particularly stiff, which was why she couldn't allow it. She wanted his hands on her too much and that was simply a stupid thing to do. Wanted comfort. Needed it badly. Even though with Neil it was only a nice gesture meant to make the pregnant doctor feel better, to her it was too intimate, too close to her problem.

"What would help would be the rest of my cinnamon roll." She picked it up, and took a seat on the stool at the kitchen counter. "And for future reference I'll pretty much eat anything sweet. And chocolate. Salad's OK, but it doesn't get any better than this." She held up the cinnamon roll, studied it for a second, then took a bite. But she still had a lump in her throat, which made it hard to swallow.

Neil seated himself next to her at the counter and pulled a cinnamon roll from the sack. "Guess this make me officially *less* boring, doesn't it?" he asked, then took his first bite.

"Some people would call it spontaneous."

"Trust me, no one would ever call me spontaneous. That was…" He frowned, exhaled a sharp sigh, then continued. "That was my brother. His life was one spontaneous moment after another. People always called him the fun one. And I was…sensible." He attempted a laugh, but it didn't mask the true sentiment.

"Gavin Thierry?" she said, her voice oddly shaky. "The one on the plaque?" Even though she knew, she still had to utter the words and hear his response.

"That's right. My half-brother, actually." Cold, distant words.

There was so much resentment bottled up in *the sensible one*. She could hear it, even though he was trying to hide it. It was there, though, and she wondered what could have been so bad between the two. "Your brother did a very nice thing for the pediatrics ward, Neil. And I'm so sorry for your loss." It was a nice thing Bryce should know when he was old enough.

Gabby's words didn't set well with Neil, though, because he dropped his cinnamon roll onto the counter, clearly not comfortable with the topic. "We hadn't been close for a while," he said, his voice flat. "For years."

Not close for years? For Gabby, this only begged more questions. Which she wouldn't ask, even though she desperately wanted to know more for her son. And for herself, since she was the one standing in the middle of the unhappy dynamic.

Lunch was pretty quiet after that. Some general chat about the hospital. Neil going back to his traditional way of eating—main food first, no spontaneity. Gabby filling up after two cinnamon rolls, no room left for salad. Throughout the whole muted ordeal, Gabby couldn't help but wonder what had happened in Neil's relationship with his brother that hadn't been resolved even with Gavin's death. She couldn't imagine that it was old childhood resentment left over after so many years. But, like Neil, she ate in silence.

After she'd had all the food she could hold, Gabby put the leftovers in the fridge, then faced Neil across the kitchen counter. "I'm going back to work with you." Staying cooped up here, alone, only made her think, and she didn't want to. At least, not about the things she needed to.

"Fine," he said, no argument.

She'd expected an argument. "That's all you have to say about it?"

A small smile finally crept back to his face, but not as far as his eyes. They were still troubled, distant. Still reflecting on sad memories. "Because I'm not in the mood for an argument, and if I said no, you'd argue. But you know what's best, know what you feel like doing, so I trust you in this. If you feel like working, work. Eric's still not feeling well, and I'm sure he'd appreciate you taking back your afternoon patients so he won't have to be quite so busy."

A cold breeze cut through their conversation. She could feel it, and it had everything to do with the father of the baby she was carrying. So, for now, her real question was answered.

No, she wouldn't tell Neil. It was a short-term solution, but it worked for the time being.

It didn't make her feel any better keeping it to herself, though, because Neil had a right to know. But the question was, would he want to know?

"Time will tell," she whispered to Bryce a few moments later, as Neil waited at the front door while she stood at the hall closet, slipping into her jacket. Yes, time would definitely tell.

The rest of the afternoon passed into oblivion, as did the evening, as did the week. She worked, she avoided Neil as best she could. And she bought baby clothes. Stacks and stacks of them. Plus she made a point of eating at a different restaurant every day...places where she didn't expect to find Neil. But he was always on her mind, always a guilt that weighed heavily.

And even after seven days of knowing what she knew, she still didn't know how to deal with it. "Life doesn't come with an instruction manual," she told Bryce one night as she was settling into bed. "And your mother just isn't very good at figuring out how all the pieces fit."

She wasn't expecting an answer, but she got one anyway, in the form of a phone call from Neil.

"Are we having problems?" he asked.

"No, why?"

"You seem to be avoiding me."

"Not avoiding you. I've been busy. And resting when I'm not." True. But also a great big avoidance.

"And you're feeling good?"

"No complaints." The conversation was so stilted, so cold she could almost see the frost on the phone.

"Want to have dinner Friday night? I'm on back-up call,

but I don't have to be at the hospital. And I have something interesting I'd like to talk to you about."

"Neil, I just…just don't know." She settled back into her pillows and sighed heavily. "I just don't get involved in…in personal situations. And right now I'm more in the mood to just be alone." That was true.

"So we do have a problem."

"It's not a problem. It's just that…" Why not just tell him? Accept the invitation, and get it over with. That way, she'd know if she had a future here, or if she didn't. "Look, let's have dinner together, OK? I'd like that."

Their goodbye was brief, cordial. And Gabby didn't fall asleep for a good two hours after it. She'd made the commitment to herself, made the promise to Neil, and now the real worry was setting in, because she did want to raise Bryce here, did want Neil to be part of his life. A week and a few days here and she loved White Elk, felt at home, felt like she could spend the rest of her life here. But all that was up to Neil, and he didn't even know it yet. And it scared her that when she was finally making plans, they could all blow away. Yet it scared her even more that they wouldn't.

"Your mother's not thinking too clearly right now," she said to Bryce, as her eyelids began to flutter shut. "But I promise you, that's only a temporary situation."

All the same, she hoped White Elk was not.

CHAPTER FIVE

THE next few days passed in a blur of patients and shopping, so that before she knew it the evening of her date with Neil had arrived. Truth was, as hesitant as she'd been to accept his invitation, she'd been looking forward to the evening ever since. Dreading it, of course. But hopeful. "They're going to be OK without us?" she asked Neil, trying to fasten the seat belt so it wouldn't be so tight. It was like her belly had doubled in size this past week. Maybe not so much in outward appearance as in the actual way it felt to her. Naturally, Bryce had picked this evening to be more rambunctious than ever, kicking, turning somersaults, tap dancing.

Neil chuckled. "The hospital will do fine without us for a few hours." He jiggled his cell phone at her. "And there's this. They have one too, and they know how to use it."

"OK, so maybe I worry too much. But if there were an emergency…"

"Calm down. There won't be."

"You're sure of that?"

"I've been on call five nights straight. All I can say is, I've been looking forward to this, so there'd better not be."

"Like we can control that part of our lives," she said on a wistful sigh as they turned onto the road leading out of the town, and headed for the winding road that would take them to the top of the older Sister.

Neil glanced over at Gabby, not sure if she was napping or simply relaxing. She'd been quiet for several minutes now, and he missed the sound of her voice. He'd caught himself thinking of this as a date off and on, then reminded himself this evening had a purpose. He was going to ask her to stay. He and Eric had crunched numbers, and decided they could afford her part-time for a while. Full-time when she was ready. He wasn't sure this was what she wanted, but he hoped it was because so many of the women were happy with her. Of course, he'd never really heard her talk about her future plans with any certainty, so he had no idea what she intended for herself. But maybe, over a nice dinner, pleasant music and a wonderful view of everything she could have here in White Elk, it wouldn't be so easy for her to turn him down.

On a personal note, he hoped she would stay, too. But that wasn't going to come into play, because she avoided the personal almost as much as he did. "We're winding through an area now where a lot of the celebrities have built their mountain homes," he finally said, more because he simply wanted her companionship than his pressing need to tell her which movie star lived where during ski season.

"I'll bet it would be nice, if I could see it," she murmured, sounding awfully contented.

"Did I wake you?"

"Did you want to?"

"Maybe."

She laughed. "Well, you didn't. I was just...relaxing.

Enjoying the night sky. In Chicago, you don't get many stars like you do out here—the kind in the sky, not movie stars. I was remembering the song my mother used to sing to me…'Twinkle, twinkle little star…'"

"'Like a diamond in the sky.'"

"Funny, but I don't think about her too often. It's always my dad that comes to mind."

"Did he sing to you?"

Gabby laughed. "Heavens, no. He had a voice like a fog-horn. Kind, gentle hands when he held a baby, though. That's one of the things I miss the most, seeing my dad with a new-born in his hands." She straightened up in the car seat, drew in a deep breath. "Did your mother sing to you?"

"She didn't have time, really. She and my dad divorced when I was still a toddler, and after she married my stepfather, Gavin's father, it seems like her time was consumed with all sorts of things. But never singing."

"Was she happy?"

"I think so. She was a nurse at the hospital, she raised two sons, took care of her husband… I think she had a good life with him."

"Did you?"

"Charles Thierry was good to me. Good man, excellent doctor."

"Let me guess…pediatrician?"

"The apples didn't fall far from the tree, did they? He was a very good pediatrician."

"And?"

"And he died when I was in med school, before Gavin had a chance to go to med school. My mom remarried a few years later, and she's living happily on a beach in Nicaragua."

"But you and Gavin got along back then?"

"Like typical brothers. You know, ups and downs. Until…well, let's just say that the adult years have been all *downs* and let it go at that. I don't want talk of my brother spoiling the evening. Especially when we have such a nice night ahead us."

Whatever had happened between them was bad. Hurtful. It made her nervous, made her feel guilty.

"Well, then, let's talk about pleasant things. As I recall, you said you had something you wanted to discuss with me? It's pleasant, isn't it?"

"I think it is, but first I want to ply you with food, chocolate, more food, more chocolate, to maximize that pleasant potential."

A gentle smile finally crept back to his face, causing her to relax. Right now, this was for the best. Soon, though, she would have to tell him everything,

"I like the part about more food, more chocolate. Bribes are good, but are you sure you can afford me, Neil?"

He chuckled. "I know the executive chef. I believe she'll let me make installment payments, if I have to." Yet, the real question was, could he afford her in the ways that counted? Because if she stayed, he was going to have to figure out just how he was going to do this. And it had nothing at all to do with the finances of the matter, and everything to do with the feelings.

"Have you ever thought about what you'd be if you quit being a doctor?" she asked him.

"Why? Are you thinking about quitting?"

Not quitting so much as making a big change, and finding a way to accommodate her new life in the meanwhile. "My life is changing. Who knows what I'll be doing a year from now, other than raising my son? I mean, as much as I love medicine, I suppose that could always be a possibility. Maybe I'll want to be a full-time mom, or maybe I'll settle in a place where my medical skills aren't needed."

"You're too dedicated to quit. You'd go crazy inside a month. No, make that a week. Isn't that why you're working now, just a few weeks away from your due date? Because you need to be a doctor, because it's part of you?"

"It is part of me. But what if I found a place where I really wanted to raise Bryce, but there was no need for my services there? Yet I was so happy being there, raising my son there, that I couldn't leave? Or what if you found a place to live that didn't need a family practitioner, but you wanted to stay there so badly it didn't matter? Maybe it's the kind of place where we *want* to define ourselves by something other than our work."

"In my case, is there a woman involved?" he asked, half teasing.

"You mean you'd give it up for a woman?"

Neil made a sound that sounded like a cross between a laugh and a choke. "Hell, no, I wouldn't give it up for a woman. I'd hope that a woman who's that important to me would understand why I couldn't give it up. I came close once, and it almost cost me everything. So once was enough."

"But she wasn't the right woman, was she? I mean, you two did get…" Gabby paused, deciding not to wander down that path. It was Neil's business, and if he wanted to tell her, fine. If he didn't, fine, too. "OK, so let me start this conversation over. What if the place where you wanted to spend the rest of your life couldn't support you as a doctor? No woman involved. Which would you choose? Your heart, or your profession?"

"Is that what you're struggling with, Gabrielle?"

"Not struggling. I gave up my job in Chicago because something much more important than anything I'd ever dreamed of came into my life. No regrets there, whatsoever. In fact, what I thought I was so passionate about disappeared when I realized that my baby needed something different than what I had. No contest. He won, and I don't regret that because I've discovered that when you love someone more than anything in the world, the sacrifices don't matter."

"So what you're saying is that it might not be a sacrifice, if you truly love the person you're doing it for?"

"Something like that."

"Are you talking about White Elk?"

"Maybe," she hedged.

"Well, when you are *definitely*, let me know because Eric and I crunched some numbers and we believe we could support you here as a part-timer for a while, with the option of expanding your duties in the future, when you're ready. That is, if you want to stay."

"But I thought you were trying to figure out a way to expand your trauma unit?"

"That, too. But we don't want to let a good thing go."

"A good thing, as in me?" Admittedly, the offer did give her butterflies because she wanted to stay. But it caused problems, too, as she couldn't give him an answer until she saw how he reacted to finding out about Bryce. Also, a little bit of disappointment settled over her, because she'd had this fantasy where he'd asked her to stay, and it was purely for personal reasons. He needed her, he wanted her. Not that he'd crunched the numbers and he could afford her, part-time. "Can I have some time to think about it?"

"All the time you need."

"And this was the reason you're taking me to Pine Ridge? To ask me to stay?" Again, she was disappointed. It was a silly reaction, because they were only colleagues. Still, she couldn't help the way she felt, and right now it was definitely let down.

"Part of the reason."

"And the other part?"

"I like your company, and sometimes it's nice to be part of a couple. I thought maybe you'd enjoy the evening out."

Gabby breathed a sigh of relief. It was not a romantic declaration or anything close to it, which was good. But hearing those words made her feel better. "I never dated very much. Didn't have time. Didn't have interest. Never met the right man. All of the above. And sometimes I wonder what I've missed out on, by making the choices I do. I know I didn't sound very gracious when I accepted your invitation, but I'm glad you invited me, because I would enjoy an evening out." Unfortunately, it was the end of the evening she dreaded.

"Are you thinking about staying here, Gabrielle? I mean, I don't need a firm answer, but I'm curious."

She shifted back down into her seat and twisted to stare at the stars again. *Twinkle, twinkle little star.* How she wished her life was simpler. "I'm thinking about all my options...keeping them open."

"And there's really no one else involved? You're not running away from someone?"

"No one else."

"So, would I be out of line if I asked about the baby's father?"

Not out of line so much as simply too late. It was a melancholy subject. "I told you that there is no father involved. We had a brief relationship. He was a very nice man, someone who was there when I needed to be involved. My dad had just died, I was lost. And for me, getting pregnant wasn't a concern because I never thought I could have children. Was told it wouldn't happen because...I'd had an injury when I was younger. It left me with a lot of scar tissue and opinion after opinion through the years confirmed that bearing children wasn't in my future. But never say never, right?"

"But the father...he's really not going to be involved with the baby at all?"

"No," she said, flatly. "And that's all there is to it." For now. She didn't want to ruin the evening, didn't want to drop the news on him, then spend the next few hours with a man who might not want to spend them with her. No, she wasn't going to do this now. In her mind, the scenario worked out in a specific way. She'd rehearsed it, and she was sticking to the plan.

"Sorry, I didn't mean to get so personal."

"Nothing to be sorry for. People are curious, and the only way you ever find out is to ask. But the good thing is, women have babies by themselves all the time. There's no stigma attached, no societal taboos, at least in this society. Doors are opened much wider these days for single mothers."

"And you'll be a very good mother."

She bristled right up. "Even without a father for my baby? Is that what you're implying?"

"I didn't say that, Gabrielle. Didn't imply it either. It's a good decision for you, I see it in your face every time I look at you. You're happy, and it shows. And so you'll know, if you do decide you want to stay in White Elk, accept my offer, and raise your baby here, you have a host of new colleagues who will support you."

She wanted him to say more. Wanted him to tell her how much he wanted her to stay. Wanted him to make it personal. But that was wishful thinking. Neil wasn't getting involved, the way she wasn't getting involved, even though her baby hormones were trying to turn this into something much more than it was.

Nothing was settled, and if anything, the offer that should have made her happy was beginning to feel like a dense, wet fog. A very cold one, at that.

"This is wonderful!" The tables were all adorned with lit candles and white roses in crystal vases. The light was low, the reflection from the candle glow giving off a very romantic overtone. Tonight was a night for lovers was what it said.

Wasted on her, of course, but appreciated all the same. "I'm not sure what I thought this restaurant would be like, but it's…elegant." Very different from the lodge look she had expected—cedar logs, stone fireplace, animal heads adorning the wall. The restaurant was refined, its menu select, its ambiance pure class. And she felt so clunky in her one and only maternity outfit—a black skirt and black sweater—and snow boots. Clunky in and of themselves. "Why didn't you tell me it was so nice?" she hissed at Neil, who was impeccable in a gray wool suit, with his black turtle-necked sweater underneath. The beauty and the…underdressed frump.

"I thought you looked fine."

The dining room was full, the singer, an older woman in a long sequined gown, kept the crowd mesmerized by her dulcet tones, and all Gabby wanted to do was sneak through to her table and hope the tablecloth was large enough to conceal most of her. "I expected a lodge dining room like the one at Laura's. I didn't know this was a world-class restaurant."

Neil laughed. "You're being too self-conscious."

"Spoken like a man," she snapped, looking down at herself. Things went well on top, started to deteriorate around her middle, were pulled pretty darned tight over her rear end, and the boots…a concession to comfort she'd found two days ago, on sale. Faux fur that looked like she was wearing a raccoon wrapped around each ankle.

"OK, so maybe the boots aren't good," he admitted, fighting back a smile. "But they'll be under the table, so no one will notice."

"Which is where you'll find me," Gabby muttered, as Neil took her by the arm and led her all the way over to the window. Naturally, he stopped at several tables along the way to say hello, to ask how someone was feeling, to introduce her to a highly styled couple he thought she should know. So, what could have, or should have, been a quick trip across the carpeted floor turned into twenty long minutes in which she knew people were turning their heads, asking questions. Pointing.

"I didn't know," Gabby explained to Angela, who hurried over to the table the instant they were seated. "And I apologize."

"For what? I'm just glad you're here. When I saw that Neil had made the reservation I decided to stay over and make sure your meal is perfect. Even though I won't be cooking it. But I did make a fabulous chocolate trifle for dessert, since I knew you were craving chocolate."

Gabby pulled her boot out from under the table. "This is what I'm apologizing for. I might have to have a double serving of the trifle to get me over the trauma."

"She thinks she's out of place." Neil set aside the wine menu and went straight to the menu of imported waters. "I told her she's fine, but she won't believe me."

Angela laughed. "He's right. You're fine. And I'm so glad you're here."

"How are you feeling?" Gabby asked.

"You're off duty, Doctor," Neil reminded her, then ordered a sparkling water from Belgium. "Time to relax, which you're not doing very well at right now."

"I'm fine, and I've got to get back to the kitchen," Angela explained. "And I've got your meal all planned, so please sit back, relax, enjoy yourself." She turned away, had a second thought, then turned back. "Dance. We have an awesome dance floor here. And I know an obstetrician who would tell you that the exercise would do you good."

Gabby gave her a scowl. "I don't dance." Angela was trying to turn this into a romantic date, and that wasn't going to work, no matter how romantic the atmosphere, the food or the music. But the smile she saw on Neil's face made her wonder if he thought differently. "I don't," she protested. "Never have, except for a couple of school dances when I was a girl, and I was terrible."

Angela scurried off to the kitchen, leaving Gabby and Neil to the discussion. "So you really don't know if you can dance, then, do you?" he asked.

"And I'm not about to find out."

"What if I asked you? Called in the gratuity you offered for the massage. Remember that?"

"I remember reserving the right to put conditions on that gratuity, so I'd have to say no."

"And you wouldn't find that a little rude, turning down your dinner escort that way, especially when a gratuity *you promised* still hangs in the balance?"

"If my dinner escort valued his toes, he wouldn't ask." She sat back in her chair and folded her arms over her chest. "So don't ask."

"What if I said that dancing is good for the baby?" His eyes positively twinkled with mischief.

"Then I'd say it's a good thing you're not an obstetrician, because dancing has nothing to do with fetal development."

"You're referring to Bryce as a fetus, now? And just when I've gotten use to personalizing him?"

She didn't answer as the waiter placed a champagne bucket next to the table. In it was a chilled bottle of sparkling water, which he served the way he would have served a fine wine. Gabby kept her eyes fixed on him while, across the table, Neil kept his eyes fixed on her—making her totally uncomfortable. Given different circumstances, this might have turned into the night he expected. But circumstances weren't different, and nothing was going to change. Or, actually, it would once the evening was over.

"Why are you staring at me?" she asked.

"I've never been this up close and personal with a pregnant

lady," he admitted, "and I'm finding it fascinating. I'll bet you don't even know how many times in any given hour you raise your hand to your belly, and smile. And it's a warm smile, one that comes from a place I'm not sure any man could ever truly understand, which is too bad, because I've always thought men were left out of the best part. It's amazing, though, isn't it? A brand-new life about to happen. We know how it happens, know *that* it happens, but it's still amazing and all the men can do is stand back and watch."

"Want to do more than watch?" she asked. "He's kicking, if you'd like to feel."

A smile spread across Neil's face as he laid aside his napkin, stood up and went to her side of the table. Without a word, Gabby took his hand and guided it to her right side where, indeed, Bryce was making himself known. Then, instinctively, she pulled up her sweater to let Neil see the little blips her baby made on her belly when he kicked. "He's one rambunctious boy," she said, surprised how intimate this felt. Normally, she hated people coming up and touching her belly like it was their right. So many people did that. Poke, prod, pat…it made her cringe thinking about all the uninvited hands she'd had on her lately. But Neil's hands, as he laid them on her bare flesh now, and felt the kick of her child in a way no one but she had before, were so gentle, so right. What surprised her was how the baby settled down almost immediately under Neil's touch, like he knew that this man was part of his life.

"You have a good way with him. I guess that's why you became a pediatrician," she said, pulling her sweater back into place as the waiter approached the table. All too soon the moment was over, and Neil was back sitting across from her, staring again, as the waiter fussed over the table, rearranging the flowers, setting aside the candle, refolding the napkins.

Gabby liked it that Neil watched her that way. In an odd

sort of way, it made her feel almost…sexy. And pregnant women were sexy. That's what she told her patients every day. But sexy had no place in *their* relationship. They weren't lovers, sharing a wonderful experience together. After this evening, after she told him the little boy he'd just felt kicking was his flesh and blood, they might not even be friends. So rather than saying anything, she took a drink of her sparkling water as melancholy slipped down over her. They had no future, no past. All they had was just this moment, which suddenly felt lonely.

Dinner went nicely in spite of the glum mood that had come on her earlier. The food was wonderful, the conversation light. Neil wisely avoided talking anything of substance, for which she was grateful, and he even managed to stay off hospital matters. Throughout the whole thing, Gabby couldn't help but wonder what it might have been like had this been a real date between two people in different circumstances. Maybe in love, or on the verge of it. But this was her lot now, and while the evening had brought on a good case of the blues earlier, she wasn't really unhappy. They were temporary, while the excitement of what was happening to her was permanent. It's all good, she decided on her way back from the ladies' room. "And things will work out the way they're meant to be," she whispered to Bryce.

She cut around the edge of the dance floor, where a dozen couples were dancing to something seductive that could have been sung by Frank Sinatra. The low tones from the tiny orchestra were so smooth and sensual, she couldn't help but slow her pace, to watch for a moment, and to listen. Which was her mistake, because Neil stepped up from behind and led her straight to the dance floor.

"Gratuity time," he whispered, as he took hold of her hand and pulled her into him as far as she could go, all things considered.

"And if I simply walked away?" She wanted to, but she was suddenly discovering that so much of her didn't want to. For a little while, it would be nice to live in the illusion that they were a romantic couple caught up in the pure sensuality of the dance. Even with her boots...and her belly.

"I'm not keeping you here, Gabrielle. I would never force you to do something you don't want to do. So, it's your choice."

Her choice...her body was already swaying to the rhythm. Swaying to Neil's rhythm. It was like she couldn't stop it. The music was drawing her in, pulling her even closer to Neil...he was holding her, they were dancing. Hands appropriate, of course. Proper dance etiquette. And she wished, dear heaven, she had on better shoes, something to help her glide more gracefully. But that didn't matter, because they took up so little of the parquet floor, dancing mostly in one small spot. Tighter together. Their proper dance etiquette relaxing into something more personal, her arms slipped around his neck as his slipped around her back. They looked like every other couple out there. So close... Her head on his shoulder now, she could feel his breath on the back of her neck. The steady in and out of it, the gentle brush of his lips...no lips. No, that wasn't his lips. Couldn't be.

Suddenly, Gabby pulled back, broke away, stared into his eyes. "I need to sit down." she said, trying not to sound as breathless as she was. Which had nothing to do with the dance.

"Are you OK?" he asked, leading her off the dance floor.

"Just a little winded. I'll be fine when I sit down."

She wasn't, though. She wasn't fine at all. In fact, she was so disquieted she wasn't able to eat a bite of the chocolate trifle Angela had sent along for dessert. "Did you kiss me?" she finally blurted out.

He looked up from his spoonful of trifle. Smiled. "I might have. Why?"

"Why would you ask me why? No, skip that, and tell me why you *might* have kissed me?"

"The moment was right. So was the mood."

"Whose mood?" she sputtered.

"Mine. Yours."

"How do you figure my mood was right?"

"Your head was on my shoulder, your arms around my neck. Since I wasn't the one who placed them there, then I figured the mood had to be yours, too."

He took another bite of dessert, and over the flicker of the candles between them she saw the pure devilry in his eyes. "I was…" Voice quivering, she cleared her throat. "I told you I didn't dance. I didn't know what I was doing."

"Then I claim the same thing. I didn't know what I was doing. *If* I kissed you, that is." A purely sexual smile crossed his face. "And that hasn't been established yet, has it?"

"I think it has."

"Did you see the kiss happen?"

"Of course I didn't. But I felt it." Had felt goose bumps rising on her flesh, too. And shivers running up and down her spine. Shivers that were still there.

"Are you sure that's what you felt?"

Oh, she was sure. But she wasn't going to tell him.

Neil scooped up a spoonful of trifle and held it across the table to her. Wiggled it ever so seductively close to her lips. And she wanted it, not because she craved the chocolate but because she craved the seduction. Or, rather, the illusion of seduction, as no man in his right mind would seduce a seven-and-a-half-months-pregnant woman. But it was so nice feeling wanted—in *that* way. And because she wanted it so desperately, she pushed herself back from the table, away from temptation. "What I felt was a man coercing me into doing something I didn't want to do, and I was just being polite, so he wouldn't be embarrassed by my rejection of him on the dance floor."

Neil laughed outright at that. His eyes twinkled, they crinkled at the corners, and he gave her the full effect of a laugh that was so contagious she couldn't help but laugh, too, at the absurdity of what she'd said. In fact, she laughed herself to tears, and took the handkerchief he offered, to dab her eyes. "OK, so maybe that wasn't really what I meant," she finally managed.

"What you meant was that you enjoyed it. Admit it, Gabrielle. You had a few nice moments out there on the dance floor when you finally allowed yourself to."

"It's been a while since I've felt like…a woman. I'm a doctor, a pregnant person, I'm a clunk in furry boots, I'm a mother-in-waiting. But a woman…"

"Believe me. Even with the furry boots, there's no mistaking the woman." And maybe he'd gone a little too far. But he'd been caught up in the moment. Smelled her perfume, held her in his arms, felt her head on his shoulder… Normal reaction, he was telling himself. He didn't date, didn't have a social life, and Gabrielle was…attractive. More like beautiful. And alone. He was only trying to befriend her, that's all. So the kiss had been a mistake, he'd admit that to himself, and deny its existence to her. Even though she knew he'd kissed her.

Truth was, he wasn't even embarrassed, when he probably should have been. Another truth was that, given the opportunity, he might kiss her again. There wouldn't be another opportunity, though, so he was safe.

But another time, another situation? He could almost picture himself involved with her. Maybe even more than involved. She was everything he'd never expected in a woman. Funny, direct, honest, smart. Little Bryce Evans was going to have himself one hell of a mother, and Neil was a little envious he didn't fit into the equation somewhere, because it was a nice equation. One he'd never expected he'd want.

"Well, right now, these furry boots are going to hike back to the kitchen and see Angela for a few minutes." She stood, then breezed by his side of the table, stopping opposite him. "Oh, and, Neil," she said, a tiny smile turning up the corners of her lips, "no kissing any other pregnant women while I'm gone. OK?"

Damn, she did make him laugh. And feel good. And, for the first time in years, feel optimistic. He watched her until she disappeared down the corridor leading to the kitchen, then turned on his cell phone and called the hospital. He'd given instructions that he wanted nothing short of a natural disaster to call him away, and at present there was no natural disaster, except, perhaps, the natural disaster he was making of the evening. Trying not to think about what he'd done, Neil slumped back in his chair, stretched legs out under the table and closed his eyes. Trouble was, in his mind's eye all he could see were his lips on her neck.

"Not a good thing," he muttered, taking a drink of the sparkling water, wishing it was something much stronger.

"You two looked good out there," Angela said.

She was taking a break, sitting in the employee lounge with her feet propped up on a low table. Gabby dropped down next to her, propped her own feet up, then compared pregnant bellies. She was carrying in a little ball in front, and an old wives' tale said that meant it was a boy. But Angela was spread out all the way around. The same old wives' tale said that meant it would be a girl.

"I felt pretty good, too. Except for the fact that I wasn't dressed properly, and my dancing shoes didn't really allow me to dance."

Angela laughed. "I'm really sorry about that. But people

come in here dressed every which way. You really don't stand out as badly as you think."

"It's a nice restaurant, Angela. I can see why you missed it, not being able to cook."

"Well, I'm going to be off on maternity for quite a while, at least three months, so at some point I'll have to get used to it."

"So who'll be in charge while you're gone?"

"My sister is coming in from Arizona to take over the kitchen, and to help me. She's a nurse. Well, she was a nurse. Not sure why she quit, but she did. So she has the time, and she also has a certificate from a culinary institute. Cooking was her first career choice before she fell in love with nursing. So, she'll be here shortly and who knows? Maybe she'll stay on and cook for me since she's saying she's not going back into nursing."

"Some people just burn out." Gabby arched her back when Bryce kicked, then shifted. "I just get comfortable in one position, then he changes, and I have to change."

"Did you ever *not* want to know his sex?" Angela asked.

"Not really. I wanted to establish a personal relationship with my baby right from the start, know who he is, call him by name. Which meant he had to be more than an it—you know how people always refer to an unborn baby as it. But I didn't want that. I wanted to know who I was bringing into this world, probably from the instant I knew I was pregnant."

"Brian calls our baby *it*. In fact, in the divorce papers that arrived this morning, he stated that I can have full custody of it. Not the baby. Not the child. Not the boy or girl. *It*." She sighed wistfully. "His charge is that we'd agreed to not have children, and I tricked him."

"Oh, Angela. I'm so sorry. I'd really hoped you could work it out."

"I did, too. He didn't. But I can do this, and I've got your example to follow. And just think. If you stay in White Elk, our children will be friends, playmates." Angela pushed herself to the edge of her chair. "So, do you know?"

"Know what?"

"Whether I'm having a boy or a girl?"

Her guesses were usually right, but she never told her patients what she guessed. "Want the test? It's easy."

Angela shook her head. "I like surprises."

"Surprises and miracles." Hers, and Angela's. "You're going to do just fine with this. I'm a pretty good judge of future mothers."

"It is a miracle, isn't it? I guess I never thought of it in those terms."

"It's always a miracle, but some miracles are different. So, since you don't want to know your baby's gender, tell your friends to buy yellow for you. It goes either way."

"If *you* were buying me a baby present, what color would *you* buy me?"

Gabby laughed. "White." Then she followed Angela to the door, where she was met by Neil.

"I think it's time to go," he said, "unless you want another dance." He actually held out his arms to her, but she waved him off, laughing.

"No dancing. No food. No more anything for the evening. It's time for this pregnant lady to go home and go to bed." Of course, the road back to the cabin was long, and she was dreading the ride. But now was the time. Neil had to know.

And she decided to tell him before they left the parking lot. "Could you wait just a minute before we leave?" she asked. "There's something we need to talk about."

"You're accepting my offer to stay?"

He put the car in neutral and twisted in his seat to face her. Thank heavens he left the dome light off and they were parked in one of the darker areas, because she didn't want to see his face right now. She was afraid it would break her heart. "I'm not sure you're going to want me to stay. In fact, you may not even want to drive me home."

He chuckled, but it was nervous. "What could be so bad?"

It was already beginning to hurt her. "I just want you to know that I'll stay here until your other obstetrician arrives, because I don't want to put my patients or your hospital in a lurch. But if you get someone in here to replace me right away, I'll go." More than hurting her, it was ripping her heart in two.

"Gabrielle, I don't understand. What's this about?"

"My baby, Neil. It's about my baby."

He was suddenly alert, sitting up straight, leaning in a little closer to her. Even in the dark shadows she could see the look of concern on his face. So she looked away.

"What's wrong?" he gasped, putting a comforting hand on her arm. "Gabrielle, tell me what's wrong, and I promise, we'll find the best doctor to fix it."

"That's the problem, Neil. It can't be fixed. What's done is done."

His grip on her arm tightened a little. "What, Gabrielle?"

"My baby's father." She took a deep breath, and swallowed. "Bryce's full name is Bryce *Thierry* Evans. Gavin is…was his father."

Neil didn't respond. Not in the next few seconds. Not in the next two minutes.

"Neil?" she finally whispered. "Did you hear what I said?"

"What I heard," he began in a perfectly calm voice, "is that, first, my brother slept with my wife, then stole her. Then he slept with you and got you pregnant."

"Your wife?" she choked. Just when she thought this moment couldn't get any worse… "Gavin stole your wife?" *Worse, had she slept with a married man?*

"He stole, she went. Whatever you want to call it." Still calm, and much more in control than she'd thought he would be, Neil started the car, and it moved forward. Slowly, though.

"Don't you want to know what happened?" she asked. "Why I…why Gavin and I…"

"I'm a doctor. I know *exactly* what happened." His voice was so chilled it sent shivers up her spine.

Angry tears pooled in Gabby's eyes. She was angry at herself for hurting Neil, angry at Neil for not wanting to hear what had happened between Gavin and her. "I didn't mean to hurt you, Neil. When I came here I had no idea you were Gavin's brother, then after I found out…it was difficult. I couldn't figure out a good way to tell you. Especially after I knew you two were estranged."

"Well, at least I know why you fainted that day."

"It was a shock."

"I guess it would be." Same cold voice. "But I do have one question. Why were you in White Elk? Gavin didn't live here."

"I'd gone to Spotswood, to find him. To tell him. He didn't know. After I found he'd died, I was on my way back to the airport, and I was tired. I just wanted a room for the night. White Elk seemed so—"

"So the relationship didn't last?" he interrupted. "You and Gavin weren't together?"

"It lasted a week. At the end of that week we knew we didn't have anything worth continuing. And I didn't know he was married. I would have never—"

"He wasn't. By the time he got around to you, he'd been divorced from my ex-wife a good year."

"*By the time he got around to me?* That's not fair, Neil. I know I've hurt you, and I didn't mean to. But you weren't part of this. I didn't know you when Gavin and I were…" She paused, drew in a steadying breath. "Gavin was a nice man who helped me through some difficult days. He wasn't some predator out looking for a vulnerable woman, the way you're implying."

As they rounded a curve, and started the descent off the ridge, Neil slowed down even more.

And didn't speak again for nearly a minute. Neither did Gabby. Instead, she looked out the window, stared up at the night sky, hoping to take some comfort in the twinkling stars, but they were all gone. The night was still, no stars, a moon that was clouding over. Maybe fighting would have been better. Neil yelling, letting out his anger. But he wasn't doing that. Wasn't doing anything at all, and that's what worried her. "So, do you still want me to work until my replacement comes?" She wasn't even going to bother asking if he still wanted her to stay in White Elk, because she knew the answer to that one.

"You do whatever you want, Gabrielle."

Frigid indifference. She hated that. But that's what it was, and she'd deal with it. She'd made promises here she wanted to keep. "Then I'll work for a while longer."

"Fine."

"And leave as soon as I'm replaced."

"Fine."

"I'm sorry he hurt you, Neil. I didn't see that side of him."

No response.

"And if I'd known..." What? What would she have done differently? Gavin had been an important part of her life, and she couldn't deny that. He'd given her a baby, and for that gift, he'd always have a place in her heart. "I'm sorry I hurt you. That's not what I wanted to happen."

"You have one hell of a way of ending a nice evening," he snapped. And that's all he said until they turned onto Aspen Loop, where, in the distance, they could see red and blue lights flashing through the pine trees. Emergency lights. Everywhere. "Damn," he muttered, accelerating just the slightest.

"What is it?" she asked.

"Nothing that's going to involve you," he said. "And I mean it, Gabrielle. You're staying out of it."

"And you can stop me?" she snapped.

"I can, and I will."

"Because you're angry with me?"

"You're damn right I'm angry. Mad as hell. Don't know what to do about it yet either. But that's not the reason."

"Then what is?"

"You're carrying my nephew. That's the reason."

CHAPTER SIX

ERIC RAMSEY was already on the scene when Neil stopped the car and got out. Gabby stayed right up with Neil, matching his fast, furious steps as he made his way over the rocky road to the guardrail that seemed to be the center of activity.

"Two vehicles involved," Eric said in greeting.

Neil was already out of his suit jacket, pulling on a pair of coveralls one of the medics had handed him the instant he'd jumped out of the car.

"One was a van," Eric continued. "Teenagers out doing whatever the hell it is teenagers do. Thank God my girls are only five." He paused, shook his head, refocused. "Anyway, the other car didn't go over. Man and woman, no significant injuries."

"How long ago?" Neil asked.

"Thirty minutes."

"Any sign of life from down below?"

"Over here," Eric shouted at the light crew, a group of volunteers whose job was to light up the scene of the emergency.

They carried portable utility lights of all kinds, which would run off the generator that was being pulled into the scene at the same time. "We need them as near the edge as we can get them." Then to Neil he said, "So far, nothing from below. The van is visible. It's hung up on a ledge down there and I have no idea if it's stable, or what we'll find."

"Anybody else down there yet?"

"Not yet. We've been prepping the scene up here first."

"OK, then. Let me go get into my harness and I'll be ready in a couple of minutes." He spun to walk away, then stopped, and turned to face Gabby. "I'm not even going to bother warning you to be careful, because you'll just do what you want anyway. But this could be a long, hard night. So take care of yourself." His voice wasn't quite angry, but wasn't friendly either, and the chill in it wasn't missed by Eric, who frowned.

"Everything OK?" Eric asked, both Gabby and Neil. He looked first at Neil, then at Gabby, then back to Neil when he didn't get an answer

"Fine," Neil finally ground out. "Everything is just fine."

Eric took that as a hint not to pursue the matter any further, opting, instead, to go to the equipment truck to harness up. Neil followed immediately. "Don't ask," Neil said, waving off his partner before Eric could say a word.

Eric tossed Neil his harness. "If I'd known your evening was going that badly, I'd have called."

"Evening was fine. The ride home wasn't."

As Neil harnessed up to go down the side of the mountain face with Eric and the others, he avoided watching Gabby, who was in the process of establishing herself in the back of one of the ambulances, pulling out various medical supplies that might be needed. It was too damned frustrating. He didn't need it. Didn't need anything but the life he'd had before she'd come to White Elk.

"Anything I can do?" Eric asked, as the two of them were about to go over the side of the mountain.

"Shoot me in the leg if I ever go near another woman."

Eric grimaced. "That bad?"

"That bad."

"Maybe you just need more practice with women."

"The only practice I need is in avoiding them."

"Well, for what it's worth, I understand you two looked pretty good out on the dance floor. Actually, I heard several interesting versions of the story."

"Already?" Neil snapped, as he checked his ropes. Emergency lights were finally directed down the mountainside, and dozens of people, all of whom knew their jobs, pressed into action as two doctors and three other rescuers lowered themselves over the side of the mountain, and disappeared down into the black abyss.

Neil liked this part of the job, the physical rigors of it, the adrenaline burst. Gavin had, too. In fact, rescues like this had been one of those times he and Gavin had worked well together. Back in simpler days. *Much simpler*, he said to himself, thinking about Gabby and trying *not* to connect Gavin to her. "See anything?" Neil called to Eric, who'd come down parallel to him, while the other three came down in the second wave.

"Maybe a headlight, but I'm not sure."

Whatever they found, it wasn't going to be good. Sighing, Neil turned his attention to getting to the bottom. But not before he gave one brief thought to Gabby. What the hell was he going to do now? She had no one, and she was carrying his nephew. The normal thing, under these circumstances, would probably be to walk away from her. But that wouldn't be the right thing, and right now he wasn't sure he wanted to do the right thing. Not sure at all. "I see it!" he shouted to Eric.

"About twenty feet down, and to the left. Nothing moving, as far as I can tell."

And he sure as hell wished he hadn't kissed her.

Aching back, cold to the bone, the first hour into the rescue had been an exercise in patience because all they'd done was wait. Neil and Eric were at the van, word was there were survivors, but so far no one had been sent up. Several others had gone down, though, to tie off the van to make it secure. It was a slow process. Gabby was frustrated and uncomfortable, and that was about her physical circumstances. The way she felt about Neil's reaction…actually, she was trying *not* to think about that.

People all around her were pitching in. It was an amazing thing to watch, because tables were set up and coffee was being handed around to rescuers and watchers alike. Blankets were coming out of car trunks and being wrapped around the shoulders of anxious parents waiting to find out if their children were in the vehicle at the bottom of the ravine. It was an almost surreal scene, because everybody seemed to know their place there. Everybody but Gabby, who decided to go lie down in the back of an ambulance while she waited, when the estimate for the first patient to be brought up turned into another thirty minutes. So she made her whereabouts known to one of the attendants, then stretched out, trying to fight off the dull, heavy sleep that wanted to slip down over her. Emotional sleep, she decided. Something to heal her dull emotional state.

But she didn't sleep. She just existed in oblivion for a few minutes, not thinking, not planning. Not asking herself the obvious questions. Eyes closed, and focused only on her breathing, maybe her mental escape lasted five minutes when all of a sudden Gabby had the distinct impression that she was being watched. When she opened her eyes and turned her head she saw him. He was kneeling next to the stretcher on which she was resting, his face only inches from Gabby's. "Who are you?" she whispered, so not to startle the child.

He whispered back. "Benjamin Tyler Janssen, ma'am."

Polite child, and scared to death. She could see that in his eyes. "And what can I do for you, Benjamin Tyler Janssen?" She guessed him to be seven, give or take a year.

Benjamin shrugged, didn't answer. Tears were welling in his eyes but not spilling.

"Were you in the accident?" He could have been. Maybe he'd climbed up the side of the drop-off on his own.

"No," he replied, his voice quivering as the tears got closer.

"Are you hurt, Benjamin?"

"No."

That was good. "Are you here looking for someone who might have been in the accident?"

"No," he answered again, as the tears finally began to roll down his cheeks.

By now, Gabby knew Benjamin wasn't going to be forthcoming with information, and if she wanted to find out what was going on, she'd have to ask the right question. Which could go on all night. Except the child was here at an accident scene, kneeling in the back of an ambulance. The doctor in her took over. "Is someone you know sick, or hurt?"

"My grandpa. He said he didn't feel so well, then he..." He sniffled, then wiped his tears on the sleeve of his jacket.

"What, Benjamin? You have to tell me so I can help him."

"He went to sleep. And he wouldn't wake up."

A whole list of possibilities raced through Gabby's mind. Stroke, heart attack, complete cardiac arrest. "Well, I'm a doctor, Benjamin, and I want to go see your grandfather right now. Can you tell me where he is?"

He nodded. "He's still in the car. We were going back to our room and he had to stop because of all the sirens."

Meaning they had been on the road to the lodge and had pulled over for the emergency vehicles. At least, that's what she hoped he meant. "You're staying at the lodge?

"Yes, ma'am. We can go hiking every day. Grandpa takes pictures and sells them to magazines."

So grandpa was a professional photographer, which meant he was probably in pretty good health. Gabby hoped that would be enough to sustain him for a while. "Do you see that black bag sitting on the stretcher right behind you?" she asked, as she scooted to the edge of her stretcher, preparing to stand.

Benjamin turned around. "Yes, ma'am."

"Well, right now, I need you to be my assistant and carry it." While she carried the bag of first-aid supplies she was taking from the ambulance—an IV set-up, a flashlight, a bag of saline solution, a blanket and some incidentals. Not much, because she couldn't deplete the ambulance. So, after stuffing everything into the pillowcase she'd been using during her much abbreviated rest, she followed Benjamin out the back of the ambulance, told one of the attendants where she'd be, then followed Benjamin through the crowd, which seemed to be growing larger by the minute.

At the edge of the scene, where the number of people dwindled, and the flurry of activity had died down, Gabby stopped for a moment to dial Neil's cell phone. She didn't expect him to answer, but she hoped that at some point he would listen to his messages. "It may be a heart attack or a stroke," she started to explain. "Won't know until I get there. But we're going down the main access road. Call me when you get my message." As she clicked off, she wasn't sure that he would.

"Do you live near here, Benjamin?" she asked, hoping a little conversation would help calm the boy.

"No. But we come here sometimes. My grandpa likes the pictures he takes here."

"And no one else comes with you?"

"Just me and Grandpa. My mom and dad stay home."

Mom and dad. That was a relief, because she'd been wondering if Benjamin's grandfather was raising him. "Well, as soon as we get your grandpa taken care of, we'll call your mom and dad." Benjamin was picking up his pace, and Gabby sensed they were nearing the car. Right now they were only a few hundred yards away from the crash site and she could still see the reflection from the lights set up all around it.

"Hurry up!" Benjamin yelled, breaking into a run.

She called Neil's cell phone again. "I think I'm at the car now." She flashed her light on it. "It's an SUV, red, with a luggage rack on top." And a man slumped over the steering wheel. "Gotta go," she said, clicking off. Then clicked right back on. "And I'm not doing anything stupid," she added, then clicked off again.

"Benjamin, what I need for you to do is stay here, on the road, and if someone comes by, wave at them, try to stop them. But don't run out in front of them." A mother's advice. And it felt right.

"Is he going to be OK?"

She wanted to make promises, but she knew better. As she opened the passenger's door and looked at the man in the next seat, her patient looked so bad she wondered if there were even any promises to make here at all. "What's his name?" she asked Benjamin.

"Ben," he said, his voice quivering as the tears started again. "Grandpa Ben."

"Well, then, let me see what I can do for Grandpa Ben." After she'd climbed inside and seated herself next to the man, the first thing she did was feel for a pulse in his neck. Nothing.

She repositioned fingers, tried again, still nothing. But on a third repositioning…a pulse! Very thready, very irregular, but it was there.

"Is he OK?" Benjamin called from the road.

If only she could twist around and be more flexible. Or at least be flexible enough to have a look in his eyes. But she couldn't. The space was too cramped and she had too much bulk, so she climbed back outside the vehicle and went around to the driver's door.

"Is my grandpa OK?" Benjamin yelled again. This time more agitated than frightened. He was expecting a miracle, and she didn't want to let him down. But the situation wasn't looking good for Grandpa Ben, and the fact that she was so limited wasn't helping.

"I have to do a few more things before I know what's going on," she told the boy. Part of her wanted to hug the child and prepare him for the worst, and part of her wanted to send him back up the road so he wouldn't have to be here if, or when, his grandfather died. She remembered seeing her mother die. It had been an aneurysm, had happened fast, while her dad had been working and she'd been home alone with her mom. It was a memory no child should ever have. But she needed Benjamin here with her, needed his help. "Benjamin, what I want you to do is make a phone call for me." She tossed him her cell phone, then opened the driver's door. "Call the number at the top of my list and tell the man who answers what I'm about to tell you…"

"Grandpa Ben, can you hear me?" she shouted at her patient. He was a big, muscular man. Curly brown hair, broad shoulders. Handsome and rugged, but much too large for her to move. "Ben, can you hear me?" No response. Not even a little stirring.

She checked his eyes. Pupils equal and reactive to light. Good. "Did you dial the number?"

Benjamin nodded. "Yes, ma'am."

Such a polite little boy. Manners were important. She intended to instill proper manners in Bryce. "Did anyone answer?"

"No," he said.

"That's OK. But you've got his voice mail, right?"

"Right."

"Then say P-E-R-L. Pulse thready, tachycardia. Respirations…" She counted for several seconds. "Normal, shallow. And BP…" She pumped up the cuff, took a listen, got nothing, took another listen, couldn't hear a thing. "Can't hear it."

Benjamin repeated her word for word.

"Mild cyanosis…"

Benjamin stumbled over those words.

"Skin cold and clammy." Over the next two minutes she made all the diagnoses that she could standing next to the driver's side, leaning in. And that's as far as she could go. Physically, she couldn't lift the elder Ben out, even with little Benjamin's help. And she couldn't even climb in and administer anything. So she was stalled here. Standing guard over a man who needed so much when she could give him so very little. "Tell him I'm starting an IV with saline." After that, she needed help or the man would die. Of that, she had no doubt. Even without the proper diagnostic tools, she knew a heart attack when she saw one. A severe heart attack.

"Ben," she shouted again, hoping to rouse him. Somewhere in the back of her mind, she saw a situation where Ben woke up and with a little help from her was able to climb into the next seat over. Easy solution—she'd drive him to the hospital. But that wasn't happening. And each and every time she felt for a pulse, what she felt was the heart rhythm of a man closer to death than he had been when she'd checked him the last time.

"The man said he's coming," Benjamin shouted.

"What man?"

"The one on the cell phone. He called back. Does that mean my grandpa is going to be OK? Is that man going to help fix him?"

"That man is a very good doctor, and he'll do everything he can to help your grandpa." She took another pulse. Unfortunately, Benjamin's grandpa was failing fast. Too fast. By the time she saw headlights coming toward her, she couldn't find a pulse at all. Couldn't count a respiration.

"He's coding," she called, as Neil jumped out of the ambulance he was driving. "And I can't get him out of the car seat."

"Get what you need from the ambulance," he said, running past her. "And, Gabby, it's just the two of us. We couldn't spare anybody else from up top. They're finally getting the kids up and it's taking every medic we have up there."

In the ambulance, she found cardiac drugs and a portable defibrillator, which she handed to Benjamin to carry over to Neil. There was also a bag to force air into his lungs and an intubation tray if the field resuscitation went that far. By the time she got everything to the road, Neil had Grandpa Ben out of the driver's seat, lying in the dirt, with the SUV headlights pointed directly on them. He was doing chest compressions, alternating them with mouth-to-mouth resuscitation. Gabby's first task was to hook the leads from the defibrillator to Grandpa Ben's chest, which she did, only to find him in ventricular fibrillation—a condition where the heart was more quivering than beating. Her second was to ready the cardiac drugs as Neil did the cardioversion—shocked the man's heart.

"Damn," he muttered, when it didn't convert to a normal sinus rhythm. "Do you know if he's had previous heart problems?"

"Don't know. I looked in his pockets and in the glove box

in his car and didn't find anything—no drugs. So I'm assuming not. And he's physically active."

"Of course he's physically active. Do you know who this is?" Neil asked, as he prepared to give Grandpa Ben another shock.

"Someone I should know?"

"Ben Gault, one of the most noted photographers in the country."

She'd seen his photos in an exhibit in Chicago last year. Impressive. In fact, she'd bought a couple of copies and hung them in her condo. Admittedly, Ben Gault's subject matter was responsible for some of her discontent. All the hours she'd looked at the nature he'd captured through the lens had made her realize she wanted more than she'd had. It had been the start of something big in her life. Suddenly, it occurred to Gabby that she'd been looking at the Three Sisters from different angles all those months. No wonder she'd felt at home here so quickly. "*The* Ben Gault?"

"The one and only."

After the drugs were pushed in, Gabby took the portable oxygen little Benjamin had dragged over, and attached it to the bag and mask to ventilate him. But the mask wouldn't get a tight seal. Grandpa Ben's face had huge contours that wouldn't meld to the mask seal, so the only other option was to intubate. Which she couldn't do, because Grandpa Ben was on the ground, and whoever did the intubation would have to get flat on their belly. Heaven knew, she couldn't do that now. So she took over chest compressions as Neil placed the tube in their patient's lungs.

"I'm concerned that he hasn't shown any signs of rousing, even before he crashed," she whispered to Neil, as he wiggled into a good position, then pulled up Grandpa Ben's chin to start the procedure. "I have no idea how long he's been this way, which also has me concerned."

"But he didn't crash until just before I got here, did he?"

"Your timing was perfect. And I was getting scared, because there wasn't anything I could do."

Neil didn't respond as he slipped the straight-bladed laryngoscope into Grandpa Ben's mouth and had a look at his vocal cords. Neither did she talk as she continued pumping on the man's chest. Her back already ached, her arm muscles were cramping up, and even her shoulders were complaining.

"You OK?" Neil asked, once he slid the breathing tube into place.

"Are you?" she asked in return.

He glanced up briefly. "I don't want to talk about it, Gabrielle."

"I think we should. I want to tell you about Gavin."

"*You* want to tell me about my brother?" He snorted. "Well, guess what? What you know about him is nothing I want to hear." On purpose, Neil turned away from Gabby as he taped the tube into place, then he took over the chest compressions and gave Gabby the task of ventilation. No more words spoken between them.

Gabby knew better than to pursue it. This wasn't the time. Neil wasn't ready. Maybe he never would be.

An hour later, Ben Gault was alive and doing better, tucked into one of the hospital's few intensive care beds, and except for a few words concerning their patient, she and Neil had said nothing to each other. In fact, the air between them was downright cold. She'd expected that, but she'd hoped she was wrong, that Neil wouldn't have reacted the way he had. "It is what it is," she whispered to Bryce, as she went to check on little Benjamin.

"Can I see my grandpa?" he asked.

Gabby sat down on the waiting-room sofa next to him, and put her feet up. "He's sleeping right now, but maybe in a few minutes we can sneak in there together and have a look, if you promise not to wake him up."

"Is he going to be better when he wakes up?"

"We hope so, Benjamin. We're doing everything we can to help him."

"He promised to take me to Hawaii with him this summer."

"You travel a lot with your grandpa, don't you?"

"When my mom and dad let me go. Sometimes they don't, but mostly they do."

"And I'll bet you love it." She was thinking about Bryce and how he would miss out on having a grandfather like Ben Gault. Her dad would have been great, like Benjamin's grandpa was. Bryce wouldn't have a father either. No men in her son's life, which was something she couldn't help. But Bryce would miss out on so much. For a while, she'd hoped Neil might be that man in her son's life, but the likelihood of that happening was so slim she wouldn't allow herself to hold out any hope.

"It's fun. I like it when we go hiking together, and he lets me carry his camera. I have my own camera, too. Grandpa Ben bought it for me last Christmas."

"I'll bet you take good pictures, don't you?"

Benjamin nodded.

"What things do you like to take pictures of?"

"Animals. I like horses. And goats."

"You like goats?" Gabby laughed. "I don't think I've ever really seen a goat in person."

"You've got to watch them," Benjamin warned seriously. "They can be sneaky."

Like life, she thought as she settled in to wait with Benjamin. His parents were on their way to White Elk and she'd promised them she'd take care of him until then. Already she was loving it, and thinking about life with her own son. *Thank you, Gavin*, she said to herself, as she slumped down and made herself comfortable.

She was a natural with the boy. They'd been chatting for an hour and she had such a way with little Benjamin that he couldn't help but watch. She would be a good mother to his nephew. He had no worry about that.

No worry…he actually had a right to worry. Before, he'd been concerned as a friend, as someone who had been growing more than fond of Gabrielle. But now it was different. He was connected to her baby in a way he couldn't have expected. Sure, he'd had moments when he'd thought about being her baby's father, thought about being part of her little family. It had been a nice thought then. Now it was totally senseless. To be honest, he didn't know how to deal with it, even if he wanted to. He had growing feelings for a woman who was carrying his brother's baby, and there truly was no solution for that.

But she would be a good mother. "I think you two can go in to see Grandpa Ben," Neil said, finally stepping into the waiting room.

Gabby looked up at him, and nodded. But she didn't smile. Didn't speak. And as she took Benjamin's hand and walked right by him, his heart lurched.

What the hell was he going to do?

Five days into his recovery, Grandpa Ben, as Gabby was used to calling him now, transferred to a hospital in Denver for open-heart surgery. He was stable, doing quite nicely, and it was time to unclog his two blocked arteries. All the accident victims from that night were coming along at various rates of recovery, some in White Elk, some having been transferred to other facilities. No one had died, a few had required surgery, there were broken bones galore, a few internal injuries, contusions, cuts and scrapes, but what could have been a disaster had turned into a near-miracle on the mountain.

And Gabby was feeling better, too. She was rested, no aching muscles. Going along quite nicely for a woman in her advanced condition. Avoiding Neil as much as she could. Which was easy, because he was avoiding her, too.

"So, are you looking for anything in particular?" Janice Laughlin asked.

Handmade for Baby had become one of Gabby's favorite places in town, not just because of the wonderful baby items but because of Janice. They'd become friends. Had hot chocolate together every day. "What I haven't really bought so much are toys, and I was thinking a nice rattle or two."

"I have something you might like in my back room. Plus, hot chocolate."

Hot chocolate. Words meant to lure Gabby through the curtains to the back room. Following Janice, she'd no more than stepped through the teddy-bear-print curtains when several women started applauding.

"What?" Gabby gasped.

"You didn't think we'd let you have your baby without us giving you a baby shower, did you?" Laura asked. "I know you've been doing your best to buy everything in Janice's store, but we all love to do baby shopping, too." She pointed to a table filled with pastel-colored packages, most of them wrapped in white and various shades of blue.

"Plus, we have an ulterior motive," Ellen Patrick said. She was one of Gabby's patients, three months along, third child. "We want to persuade you to stay, and we know Neil and Eric asked. It's nice having you here, Gabby. After Walt Graham's grumpy ways…well, if we have to bribe you, that's exactly what we'll do."

The ladies all laughed, and agreed.

"I never expected this," Gabby said. Still standing in the entryway, she was too stunned to move. "I mean, I've never…" Had friends. Not in the real sense. And these women felt like real friends to her. Fallon O'Gara, Rose Kelly, Jane McGinnis, Jackie Pennington from the hospital. Laura from the lodge. Janice and Debbi from the store. Angela. Helen, the waitress, and Catie from Catie's Overlook. Even Amarelle from the confectionary shop. And these were only a handful of the women gathered there. For her. They were there for her.

Tears welled in Gabby's eyes. "I don't know what to say."

"That you'll stay?" Angela said.

She wanted to. More than anything, she did want to stay. But how could she? "So, where's the hot chocolate?" she sniffled.

"You OK?" Laura whispered, a little while later, as everyone was busy helping themselves to cake.

"I didn't expect this. And I'm a little awkward. That's all it is."

"I think it's more than that. The cake is chocolate. Double chocolate, actually, with chocolate cream between the layers, and you haven't touched it."

She wanted to tell Laura what was happening in her life now, because maybe Laura would have some wisdom. Maybe she'd say something that would make perfect sense, make things all better. But it was Neil she really needed to talk to. It was Neil's words she wanted to make perfect sense, make things all better. But now his words were only medical. A patient consult, a recommendation, a question. Which made Gabby feel so empty, so alone. She'd never expected to miss him the way she did, but she did. In passing, in a hall, when he'd acknowledge her with the same polite nod he did everybody else, that's when she missed him the most.

"Probably just some apprehensions over being a mother. I

mean, it's getting close. The most experience I've had with babies is delivering them. Once I hand them over to their mothers, that's as far as I go. I'm on to the next baby. But I think I'm getting a little scared at the prospect of keeping this one. You know, wondering if I'm going to be a good mother, wondering if I'm suited to motherhood."

"You're suited, Gabby. Being scared is natural, having all the worries you're having happens to every expectant mother. But you're going to be great, and if we can convince you that White Elk is really where you need to be, you're going to have a fantastic network of support. Just look at all these ladies…they love you. They want to be there for you."

"You're going to make me cry again," Gabby said, welling right up.

"Want to know the cure for that?" Laura asked.

"What?"

"Chocolate cake. A great big piece."

Chocolate cake. If only life were that simple. But for a momentary fix it was perfect. And maybe that's what she needed for a while…momentary fixes, one after another. It was certainly better than trying to find a fix for the big picture.

CHAPTER SEVEN

"Do we need to cut your patient load?"

Gabby bristled at Neil's words. "My patient load is fine," she snapped. "I'm managing."

"And that's why you're holding your back, leaning to the side? Because you consider the back spasm you're having right now as managing?" He reached out to steady her as she leaned against the corridor wall, but she jerked away from him. "Gabrielle, I think you need to sit down." He was concerned. Couldn't help himself.

"I know what I need, Neil," she snapped, trying to rub the muscle plaguing her.

"Does this happen often?" His first inclination was to pick her up in his arms and carry her to a chair. But he knew exactly how she'd respond, and he wasn't in the mood to wrestle a pregnant lady into a chair, even if she needed to be there. "Can I do something for you?" A massage was probably out of the question, even though she looked like she needed one.

"You can let me leave. I'm through for the evening, and I'd like you to step aside so I can go back to my cabin."

"You're not walking, are you?" Because she wouldn't make it. In fact, right now, he wasn't sure she'd make it to the hospital's front door.

"Is that a professional question or a personal one? You're entitled to a professional answer, but not a personal one."

He bent in close to her, until his face was mere inches away from hers. "What I'm entitled to, Gabrielle, are the feelings I'm feeling. I haven't worked them out yet. And you'll have to admit this isn't a normal situation. But I am concerned about you, and about the baby. I was before I knew you were carrying Gavin's child, and that hasn't changed." He straightened up. "So I'm going to drive you home."

She looked up at him for a moment, and the fight in her eyes was so visible it was almost palpable. But suddenly she backed off. "I've missed you," she admitted.

"And I've missed you, too. I've really wished…"

"Wished what, Neil?"

"Wished things were different between us."

"Even if they were, that wouldn't necessarily make things right, would it?" Another muscle spasm hit and she gasped. "Look, Neil, I'm fine. I can call a cab."

"Or you can quit being so damned stubborn, and let me help you. I'm offering to drive you a few blocks, Gabrielle. That's all it is. A ride."

"But we'll fight," she said, the defiance draining from her eyes. "And I don't want to do that, Neil."

"Neither do I."

"Then we'll just ride in total silence, and I don't want to do that either. So it'll be best if I take a cab. But I appreciate the offer."

She started to move away from the wall, but another back

spasm caught her. Only this time she didn't fall back to the wall for support. Neil grabbed her into his arms, then whispered, "You're coming with me."

Surprisingly, she agreed. Although he wasn't going to let himself read anything into it. She needed help, and he was the one most convenient. That's all it was, all he'd allow himself to think of it. Doing a good deed. "It's not letting up?" he asked, as they made their way slowly to the front door. Every step of the way she leaned into him more and more.

Gabby shook her head. "It happens. Nothing to worry about, and I'll be fine in a few minutes." She slowed her pace as another spasm hit.

"Like hell you will," Neil said, whisking her off the floor and straight into his arms even though every fiber, strand and ounce of common sense in him was screaming *Put her down and get out of there*. But with a pregnant woman nestled in his arms who was at least as shocked as he was, it seemed he was committed to this.

"I appreciate a good chivalrous act every now and then, the way most women do," she said as she straightened herself in the passenger seat of his SUV a few minutes later. "But don't ever touch me again, Neil. Because I might have to hurt you if you do."

"With what?" He couldn't help the laugh that bubbled out of him and stayed with him all the way round to the driver's seat. Couldn't help that it didn't quit when he climbed inside and started the engine.

"What's so funny?" she snapped, trying to find a comfortable position.

"The look on your face. I think you did want to hurt me, didn't you?"

"Did it ever occur to you that I didn't need, or even want, your help, since I didn't ask for it?"

"OK, so you didn't ask, but could you walk?" he asked. "Right then, could you have taken a step without someone helping you?"

"Maybe not, but that's not the point."

"Point is, you and baby Bryce—*my nephew*—need to be off your feet while your muscles are working themselves out, and leaning against the hospital wall wasn't going to do it for you."

"And if you hadn't come in, I'd have been fine in a few minutes."

"But you're off your feet now, aren't you? So, are you feeling better?" She wouldn't admit that she was. He knew that, knew she was too stubborn to give in. He'd bet his life on it. But he liked the argument and, admittedly, had missed them since she hadn't been talking to him. Even though things weren't worked out between them, it was nice to have a little interaction with her again.

"What I'm feeling is… You know what? I don't know how I'm feeling. I don't even know what I'm supposed to feel. I'm happy, Neil. Happier than I've ever been in my life about having this baby. And I'm sorry I've hurt you. But there's nothing I can do about any of it. So that's why I don't know what to do, or how to feel."

For sure, Gabrielle was one big entanglement he shouldn't be having, but common sense seemed to go into hibernation every time she came near him. Because he was tangled up, probably in more ways than he knew.

"For what it's worth, I'm not angry with you."

"It's worth a lot," she said, practically in a whisper.

"Then I hope you can understand why I'm not…" He swallowed hard. "Not getting more involved. I can't do it, Gabrielle. I just can't do it." He wanted to, though. Problem was, he didn't know how. Didn't know if he would ever know how. And it was tearing him up.

* * *

"Neil, you're going the wrong way." This very short ride seemed interminably long. Of course she understood Neil's feelings. Understood why he couldn't get involved. It hurt, because she wanted him there with her, but she knew why that wasn't meant to be. But could they work out another relationship? One where she could stay in White Elk? One where he could be an uncle to her son?

She hoped so, but she wasn't optimistic. Although she wasn't going to give up on it yet.

"No, I'm not."

"Then why is the street to the lodge where I'm staying two blocks back?"

"Because I'm taking you to my house. I have something that just might help you in your present state."

"My present pregnant state, or my present aching-back state?"

"A little bit of both. Something my mother bought for me months ago, and I haven't had time to use."

"Which would be…"

"One of those new state-of-the-art massaging chairs. It massages back, shoulders, arms, legs, neck. Gives off a nice warm heat at the same time."

A massaging chair? Oh, my, did that sound heavenly. Her back was already much better, but the idea of spending time being massaged in Neil's chair was almost too tempting. Back in Chicago, going to a day spa for a massage had been her one indulgence. Even before she'd fallen pregnant. She would have a nice, relaxing soak in a hot tub, then have Inga and her magic hands do the massage. Of course, the hot tub was out at this late stage in her pregnancy, and Inga was still back in Chicago. But if Neil's chair worked…

Still, as tempting as it sounded, it was Neil's chair, in Neil's house, which made it off limits to her. She wouldn't let herself indulge no matter how much she wanted to. That's all there was to it. "I don't need a massage. In fact, all I need is for you to turn around and take me back to my cabin. I didn't protest when you picked me up and carried me out of the hospital, didn't protest when you put me in your car. But I'm not going home with you, Neil, and I mean it."

"Too late," he said, stopping on an uphill incline in front of what was probably the largest house in White Elk. She'd seen it from a distance on her way to the hospital, and had even wondered who lived in the house on the hill. But she'd never suspected Neil.

The house looked like a Swiss chalet towering over its neighbors below and, honestly, the more she studied it, the more she wondered about it. Neil wasn't the least bit pretentious, and she hadn't expected this of him. In fact, if she'd been asked to guess, she'd have put him in a one-room studio apartment. He was a no-fuss, no-muss kind of a man. And this house…this mansion of his was all about fuss and muss. So, what was this about? "This is yours?" she asked, just to make sure.

He chuckled. "You expected what? A cave?" After opening the car door on her side, Neil allowed her to exit on her own. No scooping her up into his arms, no other grand gestures. He simply extended his hand to her to help her out.

"Maybe not a cave." Although she could much better picture him in a cave than this. "But I expected…modest."

"Modest. An expectation of someone who never met my ex-wife. She couldn't have modest. For Karen it was all or…" he gestured to the house "…even more than all. Then, after the divorce, I got stuck with it. And I'm still stuck with it because no one in White Elk wants to buy it. So I make the best of it, since I'm not here most of the time anyway."

He walked alongside her, ready to help if he needed to, but she was steady on her feet now, no more back spasms. Which meant she really didn't need to be here. She was curious, though, and she wanted a peek inside now that she'd seen the outside. So she'd have her look around, then she'd ask him to take her home. Or call a cab. Good plan, she decided. Safe. "Well, I can certainly say it's impressive," she said as Neil punched the front-door code into the keypad.

"It's meant to be impressive. That's why my wife bought it."

"And you didn't stop her?"

"Sometimes when you're in love you overlook things. In our marriage, this house is one of the things I overlooked."

She wanted to ask what the other things were, like had he suspected his wife was having an affair with his brother? But she didn't. Right now, the mood between them was better, and she wanted to keep it that way. If they could stay cordial, the way they were now, that might work, might allow her to remain in White Elk. So, she put Neil's wife out of her head to the extent that she could as she entered Neil's wife's house.

Inside the foyer Gabby's first reaction was a gasp. Neil's chalet was palatial, decorated so elaborately and beautifully she simply stood there a while, turning in circles, taking it all in. Rococo mirrors, crystal chandeliers, Victorian furniture… So well appointed. A place to hold a magnificent Viennese ball if anyone in White Elk ever took the notion to hold one. Definitely not Neil in any way, shape or form, but impressive all the same. "Well, my compliments to your ex-wife. She did an amazing job, and I'm surprised she'd let you keep this house in the divorce settlement, since it was, essentially, her house."

"Her house, my money. And it wasn't a matter of keeping it. We tried getting rid of it, and no one wanted it. The divorce agreement stipulated that if, or when, it sells she'll get half the money, but because of the circumstances she's never pressed me on it. Don't think she will either."

Gabby blinked. Neil couldn't get away from it. What Gavin and Karen had done to him…it was everywhere. So much so, it was finally hitting her. Made her feel sad. Uncomfortable. Especially as Neil had it within him to sound so matter-of-fact about it. "But you still live here?"

"Not too often. I have an apartment near the hospital— three rooms, enough room to turn around if you hold your breath. Which is all I really need. And this place…it's only a building. No real memories because Karen and I never moved in. In fact, most of the upstairs isn't even complete."

Gabby's knees went weak, thinking about what all that meant. Karen had gone with Gavin before she and Neil had even moved into their new home. Then, by some cruel twist of fate, he lived in a flat with barely enough breathing room while this behemoth of a house stood on the tallest hill in town, mocking him.

"Back spasm again?" Neil said, as he rushed to her side and helped her down into an upholstered chair.

"Something like that," she mumbled. "Can I just go home?"

"I think you should give the chair a try first."

"It's been a long day, and I'm really tired." True, but she also wanted time to think. Alone.

"Five minutes. It if doesn't make you feel better in five minutes, I'll take you home."

This was the old Neil, the one she liked, the one she counted on. The one she wanted in ways she wasn't willing to admit to herself. It scared her being with him, and she should have insisted on leaving, but so much of her did want five minutes more because who knew when she'd ever get another five minutes with him? "Five minutes then I'm gone."

"Gabrielle, you look exhausted, and I'm worried about you. Right now, I'm the doctor. OK? And this doctor is prescribing some rest and relaxation before you do anything. *Anything*. So for once just cooperate."

She wanted to, but she and Neil both knew that would be a mistake. "There's nothing to worry about, Neil. I'm fine."

"You sure couldn't say that twenty minutes ago, could you?"

"Spasms are...spasms. In most cases they're nothing."

"Except an indication you're pushing yourself too much."

"So what are you going to do, fire me?"

"I probably should, but I still do believe that you're the best judge of whether or not you're able to work, and I'm not going to back away from that. At least, for now."

"Just show me the chair, OK? That's why you brought me here, so let's get it over with. It's supposed to rain tonight and I want to get back to my cabin before it starts."

"Well, now that you're being so cooperative..." he said facetiously.

He showed her to the den where his mother's miracle chair was sitting, showed her the controls and left her alone. The room was nearly dark, and that was just fine with her. With the mood she was in, she really didn't want any light shining on it.

Admittedly, the deep, warm massage from the chair, once it was adjusted to settings she liked, was wonderful. Maybe not as good as actual fingers...as Neil's fingers...but she found herself drifting off, in part because she was relaxing even when she didn't want to, and in part because the soothing hum was lulling her into another world. It was a peaceful world where she didn't have so many problems. "We may have to get a chair like this," she said to Bryce, as her eyelids drooped. Then she whispered, "Five minutes more," and a contented sigh escaped her lips.

"Gabrielle?"

He had such a nice voice. The nicest voice she'd ever heard.

"Gabrielle, wake up."

She didn't want to. Not yet.

"The chair recommends thirty minutes only, so I've turned it off."

But she didn't want to go. Didn't want to open her eyes.

"Gabrielle?"

She snuggled down more in the chair, and sighed contentedly. "Five more minutes," she murmured.

"Five more minutes," he said, putting a blanket over her. But this time he didn't leave the room.

This time he sat down in an easy chair in a dark corner on the far side of the room and simply watched her for the next hour, after which she finally did wake up for real.

"Neil?" she whispered in the dark.

"Over here," he said.

"How long was I asleep?

"About an hour and a half."

"And you watched me the whole time?" That did make her feel odd. Not angry. Maybe a little flattered.

"Not the whole time. Just for a little while. You talk to him in your sleep…to Bryce. I heard you murmur his name a couple of times. I'm not sure if I mentioned this before, but I like the way you talk to him."

"We're connected. He's part of me, and it would seem so odd not talking to him. To me he's always been another person. Besides, studies show that babies in the womb do hear…you know, recognize their mother's voice. It makes our connection even closer, I think."

"I think he's a lucky little boy, having you for his mother."

The natural thing here would have been to ask Neil if he wanted to be involved in Bryce's life. But she couldn't do that, for she feared his answer would bring a screeching halt to a very nice evening, and a very nice moment between them. She wasn't ready for that, wasn't in a hurry to get back to where they'd been before this evening had started. "You know, your mother has good taste in massage chairs. I think I'm going to have to buy one of these myself."

"And put it where, Gabrielle?"

His question caught her off guard. "What do you mean by that?"

"What I mean is, where will you put your chair? Here, in White Elk, or somewhere else?"

The former ache to her neck snapped right back as her muscles stiffened. "Where do you want me to put it, Neil?"

"To be honest, I don't know. I've been sitting here thinking about that. Wondering if we could continue a relationship, given the circumstances. Wondering if it would work out if you stayed."

The same things she'd been wondering for days, but hearing him say it hurt. Maybe somewhere, deep down, she'd hoped he would ask her to stay here. It didn't even have to come with a commitment to be friends or anything else. Just hearing that he wanted her here would have been nice, and now that he'd finally voiced his skepticism, she realized she wasn't prepared to hear it. Wasn't prepared to deal with it.

"I need to leave," she said stiffly, as she pushed herself out of the chair. "I hear the rain and I want to get back to my cabin before it starts to pour."

"You're welcome to use the guest room. There's no reason for you to go outside and get soaked."

"Sure there is. I don't want to stay here." She didn't want to sound angry, didn't want to sound hurt, but she could hear all of it slipping into her voice. And she could feel the untempered emotions slipping down, trying to suffocate her. It was time to get out of there, time to get away from Neil.

Time to figure out what she was going to do. No more putting it off.

"Before you leave, how about something to eat? I'll go fix you something, as I'm assuming that you haven't eaten yet."

"What is it with you?" she snapped. "One minute you're telling me you don't want me here in White Elk, and the next you're trying to feed me."

"That's not right, Gabrielle. I never said I didn't want you here in White Elk."

"But you never said you did."

"Because I was trying to be honest. I don't know what I want."

"Did it ever occur to you, Neil, that the decision has nothing to do with you? You know I could stay here, open up my own obstetrics practice independent of your hospital. And I think I have a solid enough base already to have a chance at a good practice, because a lot of people do want me to stay. They're asking. Did you know that? There are people here in White Elk who want me here." Harsh words, and she hadn't meant to say them because, ultimately, she wouldn't hurt Neil. She cared for him too much to do that. But right now she wanted some support from him, and all he was giving her was…honesty.

Honesty. Dear heaven, what was she doing, faulting Neil for being honest, when that's what she'd wanted from him all along? Maybe she was saying these things because she was hurt that what he said in honesty wasn't the honesty she'd wanted to hear from him.

"Neil, look. I…I wanted to tell you that…"

He shook his head, held up a hand to stop her. "There's nothing to say right now that's going to make it any better. I'm sorry it is what it is, Gabrielle, but I'm as entitled to my feelings as you are yours."

"I want you to be involved in my son's life, Neil. I've known that for a while. Maybe even before I knew you were his uncle."

"And that's the big chasm, isn't it? What you want, and what I don't know if I can do."

"I'll call a cab, Neil," she said, heading out of the den. She wasn't sure if she wanted him coming after her, wasn't sure that he would. But by the time she'd made it to the front door, alone, she was sure that Neil had made his choice. A choice by which she would abide. So she called a cab, then waited outside for it under the portico so she wouldn't get wet. But after mere moments, Neil joined her, put a raincoat over her shoulders, put his arm around her shoulders. Held her close. And didn't speak until the cab pulled up.

"Give me some time, Gabrielle," he said as he helped her in. "This isn't about you, or Bryce. It's about me, and I have to figure out how I'm going to work through it."

"I'll give you whatever you need, Neil," she said, then pulled the door shut. As the cab pulled away, she turned to see if he was watching her, and he was. He was standing in the driveway, in the rain, watching. And it made her heart lurch. Caused a lump to form in her throat.

Her dad had always said that the big moments in life made indelible impressions, even when you didn't know that what you were experiencing was a big moment. He said those moments, though, would stay perfectly in the mind and in the heart so they could be replayed for an eternity. This was one of those moments. She was sure of it. Because this was the moment she knew, for sure, what she'd been trying to deny.

It had been two days since she'd talked to Neil, since she'd seen him, except in passing. Two miserable days full of rain and gloom. On top of that, she was drastically cutting back her work because it was time to do that. "Does it always rain like this during the spring?" she asked Eric. He'd just finished an emergency appendectomy, and now he was sitting in the emergency room lounge, feet propped up on the admitting desk, involved in a serious relationship with a can of soft drink. Two, actually. The one he was drinking and the one he would drink when he'd finished the first one.

"This is unusual. Normally we get the spring runoff from the melting snow, but the rain is pretty uncommon."

She plopped down on one of the emergency beds, raised the head, and was perfectly happy to stay that way the rest of the day, if she could get away with it. Finally, she was pregnant-tired. Her patients talked of it, she knew it existed, but now it was her reality. She was ready to have this baby, ready to get her body back to normal. "Why two cans of drink?" she asked him.

"I don't allow soft drinks at home. Try to keep things more healthy for the twins, so when I'm here I—"

"Sneak the drinks," she said, laughing.

"What's good for the dad isn't necessarily good for the twins."

"They're amazing little girls, Eric. I've spent a little time with them when I'm visiting Janice."

"Thank you. I'm a little biased, but I think they're pretty amazing, considering the life they lead. Dad away all the time, being shifted from Laura to Debbi, and a few other ladies in town when the need arises."

"But it's about the quality of time, not the quantity. And the quality shows on the girls." The way she hoped it would show on Bryce.

"Well, it wasn't what I planned, being a single father. It's not easy, but it works out."

"I hope so," she whispered. "I really hope so."

"You OK, Gabby?" he asked.

"Tired. Grumpy. All the usual end-of-pregnancy complaints. Nothing serious, though."

"Neil's the one who's grumpy around here. Compared to him you're a sweetheart."

"Well, I appreciate the compliment, but I'm trying hard to stay on my good behavior right now."

Eric chuckled. "Have you figured out whether or not you want to stay? I know there's a lot of sentiment to keep you here."

"Thanks to your sister. I think Janice's leading the campaign. But since you have another obstetrician coming in shortly…"

"Plans change, Gabby. We only have a temp coming in, no firm commitments yet from anyone who wants to stay. So if you want the position…"

"How does Neil feel about that? I mean, does *he* want me to stay?"

Eric shrugged. "He's not objecting."

That was a surprise, actually. It was also a little bit hopeful, but she wasn't going to read anything into Eric's interpretation of Neil not objecting, because that might not be the case at all. Maybe he wasn't objecting outright because he wasn't yet ready to tell Eric the reason he didn't want her here in White Elk. "Well, I'm thinking about it. But I haven't decided anything for sure yet."

"But you haven't decided against us, have you?"

"No," she said. "I haven't." In truth, the decision would be Neil's. But it wasn't her place to say that to Eric. A deep sigh of discontent escaped her, and she shut her eyes for a moment.

"Maybe I should have a look at you, Gabby. I know that Neil had Walt come in a few days ago to check you, but since you're getting so close to your due date…" Before she answered, he stood, and grabbed a blood-pressure off the table next to the exam table.

Automatically, she extended her arm while he wrapped the cuff around it. "The first eight months went so fast, but the last few weeks…"

He chuckled. "Just like the twins and Christmas. They're

fine for fifty weeks of the year, but those last two weeks…
Hell for them, worse for me. You'll find out."

Her blood pressure was normal. So was everything else.
"Any contractions yet?" he asked, as he put away the blood-
pressure cuff.

"A few. False labor. Nothing serious." Which was very
common. Many women lived with occasional contractions for
weeks, sometimes even months before they delivered.

"And you're sure you're up to seeing patients? Because we
can spread out your duty between all of us."

"As it is, everybody's already taken over my routine patient
load. I'm only following a few patients on a regular basis right
now, and I'm fine with that."

"Neil and I can take over."

"And I'll ask you when I need that. But I want to continue
working. Right now, it's only a few hours a week, but it makes
me feel…useful. And to be honest, I don't know what I'd do
with myself if I didn't have anything at all to do. I'm not
exactly the type who can be idle."

"That's what Neil keeps telling me."

"He does?"

"Honestly, I've wanted to put you on leave, but Neil keeps
saying you should be the judge of when you do that."

It was such a simple thing, having Neil stand up for her.
But it warmed her heart. "I won't put the baby at risk," she
said, as Eric started to hook up the fetal monitor. But he was
interrupted by a phone call, one where he didn't say a word.
When he clicked off, the frown on his face told Gabby that
the news wasn't good.

"An emergency coming in?" she asked.

"Not exactly. At least, not right away. But the levee up at
the mouth of the valley isn't holding well. They've got engineers up there right now, who are saying that the compromise

could endanger the whole area because the breach, coupled with all the rain, and the snow runoff, puts them in imminent danger of flooding. I think we're about to have to evacuate, Gabby."

"The hospital?"

Eric shook his head. "Probably not. It's built high. But White Elk would be in the way of a flood if that's what happens. And the engineers are pretty sure that's what's going to happen. So, I've got to get home, make sure the twins are safe with my sister. Then I'll come right back and start mobilizing a medical team to stand by. I'll call Neil and let him know, but if I don't get through…"

"I'll tell him," she said, sitting up. "You just go."

She didn't have to tell him again. Eric turned and ran out of the emergency department like a man possessed. He was. He was a man going to protect his children, and she knew exactly how that felt because nothing, but nothing, would stop her from protecting Bryce.

"You need to get out of here, Gabrielle," he said, his voice calm. But calm wasn't what he was feeling, not with Gabrielle still here. She needed to be safer. He had to make sure she was taken care of.

"But we're short-staffed, with Eric gone."

"And you're not approved for emergency duty any longer."

"Do you *really* think I'm going to do something to put my baby in jeopardy? I wouldn't do that, Neil. But you do need another doctor here for a little while."

Another doctor, yes. Gabrielle, no. The need to protect her from the flood was becoming so urgent it surprised him. Right now, getting Gabrielle to safety was all that mattered. "Just leave here," Neil ordered. He fished through his pocket for a set of keys, then held them out to her. "Go to my house. I won't be there because I do have to stay here, but it's the highest spot in White Elk." With his responsibilities, that was all he could do.

"I'll be fine at my cabin."

"See, that's just it. You might be fine at your cabin, but you'd be better off at my house, and you're just too damned stubborn to listen to me. So let me put it to you in a way you'll listen—my house will be safer *for Bryce* than your cabin. And depending on how bad the flooding gets, you might be holed up there several days. So you tell me, Gabrielle. How well protected, and accommodated, do you want your baby to be?"

"That's not fair," she snapped, grabbing the keys from his hand. "You know I'd be perfectly fine at the cabin."

"But you'd be even better at my house. More amenities, if nothing else. And Lester's going to drive you. I'll call him, and by the time you get to the parking lot he'll be there waiting for you."

She started to walk away, angry. But ten steps later she had a change of heart. Neil was only trying to take care of her. He'd thought of her safety before anything else, and here she was resisting him. She didn't want to. But she was so afraid of giving in, because if she kept doing that—and giving in to Neil was the easiest thing to do—eventually it would rip her heart in two. Putting up the barriers the way she did didn't get her any closer to him, but it didn't drive her any further away either. And that's all she was allowing herself to hope for right now, not to be driven any further away. So she spun around and drew in a deep breath. "Thank you," she said. Simple words. But they brought a smile to Neil's face. A beautiful smile that would sustain her.

"You take care of yourself, Gabrielle. I'll call you when I can."

"Please, do that."

Ed Lester chose that moment to run down the hall and motion for Gabby to follow him. Another lingering moment with Neil would have been nice, but that was also the moment Neil disappeared into the emergency department.

But she had his smile imprinted in her heart as she followed Ed into the rain. For now, it was everything.

CHAPTER EIGHT

TWENTY-TWO hours cooped up now, and for most of those hours she'd stared out the window, watching the rain come down steadily, paced the halls of Neil's house, fighting the boredom, then stared out the window some more. She wasn't going completely crazy yet, but she was so restless she was ready to jump out of her skin. Being alone in Neil's huge tomb of a house was making her feel safer, but it was also reminding her just how alone she was, isolated up on the hill away from the flowing waters in the road down below. It was a lovely house to look at, and to explore the first six or seven times she'd explored it, but the emptiness around her was almost palpable. No wonder Neil didn't spend much time here. His home, every immense nook and cranny of it, had all the warmth of an institution. And she was so lonely here she wanted to cry.

She wanted Neil.

But she was glad to be there in spite of her glum mood. Glad, and even encouraged that Neil had thought of her safety above everything else. And, sure, she'd much rather have been working at the hospital alongside him, but that was all behind her for a little while. It was time to take care of herself, and get ready for the inevitable. Just thinking in those terms made her boredom easier to bear because when she thought about Bryce, everything fell into its proper place. He was going to be here soon and her *only* plans now were to deliver a healthy baby and see what life had in store for the two of them. Or the three of them, if Neil wanted to be included.

"We'll make all the decisions in due course," she told Bryce. "Whether we'll be staying here for good or going back to Chicago and regrouping. But it's going to work for us, no matter what we do. Whatever it turns out to be, it will be good. I promise you."

Reports coming in on the radio said that some of the villages farther down the valley were being fully evacuated now, and while White Elk wasn't at the same high-level risk, the flood of rushing water in the street was a concern to her. It made her feel even more trapped because now, even if she wanted to, she couldn't get out. She didn't have a car there. "It would have been nice having Neil here with us," she said to Bryce. He'd have been good company, and on a purely medical note she'd have felt safer. All the same, the last time she'd talked to him he'd said the hospital was going crazy. People with nowhere to go were stopping by. Minor injuries were starting to trickle in, too. There were people everywhere, simply loitering.

"It's good that he calls," she told Bryce. "And we like his voice, don't we? It makes us feel safer." Made her feel better too because it was soothing. Now that her real contractions were coming, she craved that comfort. She hadn't mentioned her labor pains to him yet, because she wasn't particularly concerned that four or five an hour were going to lead to anything any time soon. They were a beginning, though. Her new life reminding her that it was just about ready to start. Of course, she was still a few weeks away from her due date, and had no reason to believe Bryce's arrival was at hand. Women often had sporadic labor pains in the last couple of months, so she hadn't triggered the alarm that she was about to give birth all alone in the house on the hill, because nothing indicated that was going to happen.

"You're just reminding me that I'm not alone," she told Bryce, as another pain hit her while she was on her way to the front window to stare out yet again. This time she saw someone coming up the drive, in a truck that was well able to navigate the eighteen-inch flood waters down below.

The truck came to a stop at the top of the hill and the driver got out—someone dressed in a bright yellow rain slicker. A woman, Gabby guessed from the person's small size as the figure ran to the passenger's side and opened the door.

The passenger was Angela! Was she in labor? Was her baby picking the worst possible time to make a grand entrance? As she pulled open the door with one hand, she placed her other hand on her belly. "Don't you go getting any ideas, you hear?"

The woman in yellow stood back as Angela ran into the house. "Neil told me you were here all alone," she said, shaking out of her wet raincoat. "He thought that since we were at a higher elevation than this place, we'd be able to get here better."

"Why?" Gabby asked, taking Angela's raincoat and waiting for Angela's friend to shed her slicker.

"Because he didn't want you to be alone. When he finally got through to the resort, he said he'd been trying to call here for hours. But the phone lines are cutting in and out all over the place. Anyway, Neil said that you were here all by yourself and asked if there was any way I could get to you. I told him I was on my way, and that my sister would come with me."

"And he didn't tell me?" Gabby said.

"He tried calling you. We tried calling you. The wires are crossed or something, because it sounded like some kind of party line with several people talking. Oh, and I'm Dinah Corday, by the way. Brand-new to town, and not impressed with your weather."

"I'm not impressed with it either," Gabby commented, picking up the house phone and trying to dial out. No dial tone, though. So she tried her cell phone, and it started to ring, but cut out almost immediately. "So it's just the three of us, stranded here without communication?"

"My phone's working, off and on," Dinah said.

Dinah didn't at all resemble her sister, Gabby noted as the three women fixed hot tea and settled into Neil's den, which Gabby had decided early on was the only truly comfy room in the house. It was decorated for a man and she imagined Neil having it done for himself.

Sipping tea, wishing there was some hot chocolate in the house, she studied the sisters. Where Angela was small, Dinah was tall, statuesque. Angela's brown hair was cropped short, while Dinah's auburn locks waved halfway down her back. Their eyes were the same, though, and that's where Gabby saw the resemblance. Dark brown, feisty. "Well, it's a big house and you're welcome to anything in it," she said, then laughed, "even though nothing here is mine. So, aren't they going to need you to cook up at the ski resort?"

"My whole kitchen staff is in, running all over each other," Angela replied. "I put my sous chef in charge and, to be honest, I was glad to get out of there. People from all over the area are trooping into the lodge, trying to get away from the floods, and it's a madhouse. Too many people."

Relaxing, Angela put her feet up on the sofa and settled back into the pillows. Within a minute, she was sleeping like a baby.

"How's she doing?" Dinah whispered.

"All things considered, good. I know she's had a lot to deal with lately, but she's managing."

"I'm glad you let her go back to work. Even the little bit she's doing means everything to her."

"Like I keep saying, pregnancy's not an illness, and it shouldn't be treated like one."

"Well, I'm glad she found you. I think if Dr Ranard hadn't asked her to come and stay with you, she would have anyway. She really wants you to deliver her baby, and she's been worried that with the flood…"

Gabby flinched under a contraction, trying not to be obvious about it, but Dinah caught on right away.

"When are you due, Gabby?" she asked.

"Not for a while."

"So are your contractions Braxton Hicks', or did I just see the real thing?"

"Sometimes it's hard to tell the difference."

"Unless you're an obstetrician." She took hold of Gabby's wrist to take a pulse. "Your pulse is a little fast."

"Just tired. That's all."

"Tired, and in labor?" Instinctively, Dinah positioned Gabby's legs on the sofa, then propped a pillow behind her head. Next came the quilt. "And have your waters broken yet?"

Gabby shook her head. "I've still got almost three weeks. And I've been having false labor for a little while."

"And unless I'm mistaken, I'm counting your false labor at one contraction every six minutes. Could you be a little off on your due date?"

Not even by a minute. She knew the exact moment of her conception because that had been her first time with a man in...well, forever. As well as her last time. "Due date is right on."

"So you're just going to deliver a little early."

All of a sudden, a sharp pain nearly split Gabby's belly in two. *This wasn't a false alarm.* And those pains she'd been having right along were the warning. Suddenly, she was excited. And frightened. And she wanted her dad. But most of all she wanted Neil.

Desperately.

"It's time," she finally confessed. "I've been hoping I was wrong. But you get to a certain point where you can no longer deny the obvious, and the obvious for me is that I'm going to have a baby, probably before the flood waters recede."

"Well, your timing's not very good, is it?" Dinah said, pulling out her cell phone. She searched for a signal in the den, couldn't find it, so she went to the lobby, which had a higher ceiling, and dialed the number Angela had given her for Dr Ranard.

The reception was crackly, but he did answer.

"You're the doctor?" she practically shouted.

Neil had no idea who was on the other end. The number meant nothing to him, and he could barely hear the voice. "Yes," he answered.

"Gabby...labor..."

"What?"

"She's in labor."

"Gabrielle's in labor?"

The answer sounded like yes, but he couldn't tell for sure. And as he tried asking a second time, the line went dead. "Damn," he muttered, running into exam four to Eric. "She's gone into labor, as best I can tell."

"Gabby? Did she call?"

"No, I think it might have been her friend, Angela. She's up there with Gabrielle now."

"Then I think you'd better get going," Eric said. "Take the back road. It's at a higher elevation, shouldn't be a problem if you use my truck." He tossed the keys over to Neil.

"You going to be OK here?" Neil asked, already shrugging out of his white coat.

"Just go," Eric said impatiently. "For once, something besides this damned hospital should come first."

Ten minutes later, on the road, he could barely think straight, he was so crazy with worry. Eric's truck, a large, sturdy four-wheel drive, would get him through the muddiest of back roads without too much problem. *He hoped.* On his way out, he'd stocked it with every medical supply he could grab in two minutes, then left the mayhem of the hospital to the rest of the staff. Angela's sister was a nurse, Angela had told him earlier. But he wasn't going to have her go through this without him.

Of course, Eric had already guessed Neil's feelings for Gabrielle. Nothing had ever been said about it, but Eric had accused him of wearing his heart on his sleeve these past weeks, and that was probably the case. Even when he was avoiding her, or when she was avoiding him, he couldn't avert the glances he fought too hard to tame, couldn't deflect the longing stares he tried to deny himself, and failed so miserably to do.

He'd wanted to convince himself he didn't have feelings, wanted to convince himself that he didn't want her. But he did. There were no more denials here. Not even about the fact that she was about to deliver Gavin's baby.

That thought caused Neil's grip on the steering wheel to tighten as the truck wheels spun in a wash coming down off the side of the mountains, flowing straight across the road. Damn, he hated going so slowly. But doing something stupid, like speeding up, would get him stranded up here while

Gabrielle was less than a mile away, having her baby. *Without him.* So he had to be steady, had to keep his head.

Dear God, you'd think it was his baby she was delivering, the way he was feeling. The way he was acting.

Admittedly, he was jealous. The perfect scenario would have Gabrielle pregnant with his child. He'd thought about it that way, tried blocking it out as that would never happen. But he'd also thought about a future where he and Gabrielle and Bryce were a family in the ways that mattered.

Except he'd been such an idiot lately. A great big idiot, blaming Gabrielle for something that wasn't her fault. It didn't matter right now, though. Nothing did, except getting through.

Suddenly, his cell phone rang, and he looked at the number. Eric. Damn. He'd been trying Gabrielle but not getting through. He'd hope this was her… "Yeah," he said, answering his phone.

"You can get down Canyon Circle," Eric yelled to Neil over the bad connection.

"What?"

"The Canyon Circle. I heard…open…may be passable."

"Is it going to hold?" It was at risk to wash out, and the last thing he needed was to get stranded up there. But if it held, it would be a shortcut. It might give him as much as fifteen minutes.

"What?"

"Eric! Is it going to hold?"

"Not sure…possibly." The connection cut out.

Sighing, Neil turned down a road that looked more like a wide trail, cursing the mud, cursing the weather, cursing the road. It was passable, but barely. It would take him straight to Canyon Circle, though, unless it washed out down the way. Which, unfortunately, it did. But before he got that far he made another turn onto the old national park trail, and spun himself straight into a ravine of mud, bringing an abrupt end to his trip by truck. Nothing that he could do out there, by himself, was going to get the back tire out of its rut.

"Damn," he muttered, gathering up as many supplies as he could carry. "Why the hell couldn't this be easier?"

The only answer came in the clap of thunder overhead as he started his way down the trail on foot, alternately slipping, then sliding where the trail washed out, most of the time managing to stay upright. Once his foot slid out from under him and he went straight down, still hanging on to his medical bag. Another time the bag flew out of his hands as he went down, and landed in a thicket of budding branches nearby. Luckily for him, it stayed latched, so once he'd pulled himself from the mud yet again, he grabbed his bag and continued his downward trek, slowing up a little for fear that if he injured himself, or ruined his medical kit, he might not be able to give Gabrielle the help she needed.

That's all this was about—helping Gabrielle. So for the next several minutes he grumbled about his slow pace as he sloshed through the many rivulets and washouts, but he kept it slow all the same until he reached the rear of his house. Pausing briefly on his patio, he phoned Eric to let him know that the back road wasn't good enough to get through without a lot of walking, and that he'd find his truck up there on the high ground at the trail head, stuck for the duration of the bad weather. Then he braced himself for what he had to do and headed straight through the back door. "Gabrielle," he called, as his rubber boots squeaked on the floor tiles, dripping mud in a trail behind him.

"She's in the front room," Dinah said, taking the medical kit from his hands and handing him a bath towel.

"You must be the nurse."

"Dinah Corday. Used to be a nurse, now I'm about to be a professional chef."

Nice smile, Neil thought, heading through the hall. She seemed competent, whether nurse or chef.

Entering the formal living room, he stepped inside the doorway and simply stared at Gabrielle. She looked…calm. Much more than he was, actually. And she was happy. "I expected something else," he said, as Dinah rushed around him and wrapped the blood-pressure cuff around Gabby's arm.

"What?" she asked.

"Maybe a little screaming. With what I had to drive through to get here, screaming would have been good because that's what I've been doing for the past twenty minutes."

Gabby laughed. "I don't think I'm a screamer, but how about a good frown?" With that, she scrunched up her face, held the pose for a second, then started laughing again. "I'm fine, Neil. Really. And you're the one who looks like he could scream." She pointed to the little pile of mud that had dripped off him. "Or could stand a good shower."

He glanced down at the mud puddle, a brown blotch standing out against the red hues of his ex-wife's favorite antique oriental rug. How appropriate that he ruin it in service to a woman he'd finally let himself love. "You just can't keep yourself out of trouble, can you? I mean, I sent you up here to keep you away from all the medical action, and now you're the center of the medical action. What don't you understand about keeping out of trouble?"

"Blood pressure's fine," Dinah said, next taking a listen to Gabrielle's belly, an oddly intimate procedure he wished he were doing.

"I'm glad to see you, Neil. I really wanted you here…"

"Did you?" he asked, looking straight into her eyes. "Did you really, Gabrielle? After the way things have been between us these past weeks…" He glanced at Dinah, who was obviously trying to make herself inconspicuous in this clumsy moment, then glanced back at Gabby. "I wasn't sure what you wanted."

"We need to have a talk, Neil. There are some things I should tell you, and…"

Another contraction gripped her, the hardest one yet. Immediately, he took her hand in his muddy one, and held it for several seconds as she nearly squeezed the blood out of it. "You've got a lot of strength for a pregnant lady," he said, shaking back the circulation once her contraction had subsided. "But I've still got a few more fingers for you to break if you need to, so we're good."

"I'm really happy you're here," she said, relaxing back on her pillows. "Even if Walt Graham had managed to drift in on his canoe, I'd have chosen you. And right now you've got about five minutes before I have another contraction, so maybe you'd better go take a fast shower, because yours are the only fingers I want to break."

"Are you sure about that, Gabrielle?" Their eyes met briefly, and he saw the answer there, the answer he wanted from her. But she glanced away so quickly, so awkwardly, it gave him cause to doubt again. It was her feelings for him he doubted, though, not his for her.

"What I'm sure of, Neil, is that you can't be part of this without a shower first, and I do want you to be part of it. So, go. Get yourself cleaned up, and come back ready to meet my son, because he's ready to pop out to meet his uncle."

As much as she wanted him here, it broke her heart just looking at his face…his beautiful, muddy face. She so desperately wished that Bryce was his son. That had been the fondest wish of her heart for a while now, one that she was only now able to admit. But what was done was done. In all honesty, she wouldn't change it, because one thing different in the whole sequence of events could have meant she wouldn't have Bryce.

It was a bad situation, and such a pervasively painful one she wasn't sure the hurt could ever fully heal. That was the sadness she saw in his eyes every time she looked. Yet Bryce was on his way now, and all the feelings, all the answers would have to come later.

"It's Gavin's baby?" Angela whispered, as she entered the room.

Gabby nodded. "Before I ever knew Neil, Gavin and I…" Another contraction grabbed her, much faster than it should have, and this time Angela surrendered her hand. But Gabby refused it, clutching at a pillow instead. "Go tell Neil it's happening…now."

"Just one more push, Gabrielle. That's all I need. One more push and you're a mother!"

She was exhausted. This was harder than she'd ever imagined it would be, and with no pain relief…

"Bear down, Gabrielle, and push."

Neil sounded so calm, so assured. And she was anything but assured right now. All her medical training down the drain, she was any other woman in the throes of delivering a baby, and that's all that mattered. "I'm pushing," she forced out, as Dinah propped her up to a near sitting position and held her there while Angela busied herself wiping a cool rag over Gabby's face.

"Breathe," Dinah said. "Come on, Gabby. Take a deep breath, then push that baby out."

"He's waiting for you, Gabrielle," Neil prompted. "Bryce Evans is waiting for you."

Bryce Evans… The men in her life passed before her eyes…her father, her son, Neil, even Gavin…as she bore down for one final time. Then, suddenly, it was over. Bryce was here. She was exhausted, happy… "Let me see him," she said to the deathly quiet room. "My baby…"

Dinah eased her back into a flat position, then hurried to the end of the bed—Neil's big king-sized bed—and Angela immediately stepped away. Went to the other side of the room, slumped down into a chair. Which was when the cold chill hit Gabby, spreading its icy tentacles through her veins, bringing to bear a terror like she'd never known could exist.

"He isn't crying," Gabby gasped, fighting to sit back up. Thrashing wildy, she was trying to toss off the sheets covering her. "Neil, he isn't crying! What's wrong?"

Even after Gabby rolled onto her side to see, she couldn't. Neil had taken Bryce to the other side of the room, to a dresser, and Dinah was with him, purposely obstructing Gabby's view. "What's wrong with my baby?" Gabby screamed, fighting to get up, even though she was too weak.

Dinah rushed back to the bed and gently pushed Gabby back down. "Look, Gabby. Neil's working on your baby right now. He's not breathing too well…"

"Did he aspirate?" Gabby choked.

"I'm not sure," Dinah said. But from the look on her face, Gabby knew better. It was the look she saw on her staff when a baby was born with a serious problem. Or a stillbirth.

"Is he alive?" she screamed, her voice so broken it didn't sound natural. "Neil, you've got to tell me, is he alive?" Neil's back was to her. She could see him working, bent over the dresser and working. But from the bed she couldn't tell what he was doing. "I've got to get to my baby," she said, suddenly launching herself up. But Dinah stopped her again.

"Gabby, let him do what he has to do."

"There wasn't a problem," she cried. "Never was a problem, and I've had so many tests, just to be sure." She rose up, watched. "Is that CPR? Is Neil giving him CPR?"

"Look, Gabby, I've got to go try and make a phone call. Do you hear me? I've got to leave the room for a minute, but

I need for you to stay where you are, and be calm. Will you do that for me?"

A million things were running through her mind, none of them good, none of them that would allow her to be calm. "I want to hold him," she whispered. "Please, I want to hold him."

"Gabby, you've got to leave Neil alone now." That was Angela. She was huddled in her chair, looking scared to death. "He knows what he's doing, and you have to trust him. So, please…"

Gabby nodded. But she didn't lie back. Couldn't take her eyes off Neil's back. Couldn't *not* watch him fighting to save her son's life.

"I'll be back in a minute," Dinah reassured, then ran from the room.

"Fight for him, Neil. You've got to fight for him."

He didn't answer, but she knew he was. Neil could do no less.

"Is he responding?" she finally asked, then watched Neil's body language for an answer. But saw none there.

"He's alive, isn't he? Neil, please say something. Anything!"

"He's alive, Gabrielle. But cyanotic. And he's struggling."

She nodded. At least now she knew. "Breathing at all?"

"Some, but not sufficiently."

"Any guesses?"

This time he didn't answer. Rather, he looked up as Dinah ran back into the room. She was soaking wet. "I finally got through to a woman named Fallon O'Gara, a nurse practitioner. Had to go halfway down to the road to get a signal, but she said to stay here, that she's sending someone named Eric in with oxygen and an IV set-up. It's too bad out there to attempt any kind of transport before we've stabilized Bryce."

"Damn," Neil muttered. "Three lousy miles to the hospital, and I can't get there."

Dinah laid a reassuring hand on his arm. "Your medic will

get here," she said. "Fallon told me he does mountain rescue, so I'm betting he'll be here sooner than you think."

He nodded gravely. Didn't speak. And that wasn't missed by Gabrielle, who'd finally managed to sit up and swing her legs over the side of the bed. One way or another she was going to get to her son. He needed her. She knew it. Could feel it deep down. So she pushed herself up, wobbled, and fell back. By the time she hit the bed, Dinah was at her side, ready to push her all the way in.

"You've got to stay strong for him," she said as she pulled the blanket up over Gabby, who immediately kicked it away.

The blanket meant she was permanently in bed, down for the count. Not having it on her meant she could get up, could get to her baby when she had to. "I have to see him," she said, this time her voice not quite so adamant. It was all beginning to sink in. Bryce was in trouble. Truly, honestly in trouble. But she trusted Neil to save him. "Please, before you take him away, I have to—"

"We won't take him anywhere before you see him, Gabrielle," Neil said. His voice was so tense it sounded as if it would snap in two. "Or hold him. I promise. But you've got to promise me that you'll be still."

She hated that promise, hated what was happening, hated more than anything that she was so helpless. So it was a hard promise to make. But she did, only because it was Neil who asked her.

For the next few minutes Neil worked on Bryce, and Gabby stayed in bed, watching everything and seeing nothing. But then, after the longest time of her life, she heard…a baby's cry. It wasn't strong. In fact, it was the cry she so often heard from a very sick baby. But it was Bryce, and he was alive, and crying the most beautiful cry she'd ever heard in her life.

"Do you want to hold him?" Neil asked, finally turning

around. In his arms he held a bundle wrapped in a brown-and-blue Argyle sweater.

"Yes," she cried, pushing herself up in bed to receive her son.

"Just for a minute. He's still not doing very well." Neil walked slowly toward the bed, never for a second taking his eyes off Bryce. Then he bent, and handed him over to Gabby. "Bryce, this is your mother, and she's awfully worried about you."

Tears of joy, and fear, streaked down Gabby's cheeks as she took her son into her arms. He was a good size, and so beautiful. But he was struggling. His tiny chest was fighting so hard to take in breath, and when she put her fingertip to the pulse in his neck, she could feel his heart beat far faster than it should. And his lips…his precious little lips were blue-tinged from a lack of oxygen. So was his skin. He *was* breathing, though, and his heart *was* beating. Where there was life, there was so much hope, and for the next few minutes, as she cradled Bryce to her chest and told him stories about his grandfather, she hoped. Dear God, she hoped.

Neil looked down at his hands. They were shaking. So far, it was a miracle that Gabrielle's baby—his nephew—was still alive. Considering that he had no equipment, no oxygen, no IV…it was the power of love and sheer determination. That's all it could be. "He's doing a little better," he said, thirty minutes into the ordeal. "Pulse rate has come down a little, and he's breathing better." Not good enough, but enough to offer some hope.

"I know," Gabby whispered. "He's a real fighter."

He might be a fighter, but if Eric didn't come soon, Neil wasn't sure how much longer the fight would hold out. "Just like his mother," he whispered. He was sitting in bed with Gabrielle, his arm around her shoulders to support her, his eyes never once off Bryce, lest a change occurred that

Gabrielle might miss. He was a beautiful boy. And he looked like Gavin in some ways. But he also favored Gabrielle. Bryce would have her smile, he guessed. He hoped.

"Neil!"

It was Eric. Eric, a former pediatric surgeon. Eric, the one who would make the real diagnosis and figure out what to do. Neil suspected the problem was something to do with the heart. The symptoms were all there, and with the proper diagnostic tools he was fairly certain he would discover transposition of the great vessels, where the two main arteries leaving the heart were reversed.

Normally, blood from the heart's right ventricle was carried by the pulmonary artery to the lungs, and blood from the left ventricle was taken by the aorta to the body. In the case of TGV, it was just the opposite, leaving the oxygenated blood meant to circulate through the body being pumped back into the lungs.

This wasn't something Neil could treat because he wasn't a surgeon. But Eric was. And for once Neil was grateful that their practice had such a pediatric influence. "Up here. My room."

Eric flew through the door, headed straight to the bed, and stopped short when he encountered Dinah Corday there. "You!" he snapped.

"You!" she snapped back.

"You two have met?" Neil asked.

"No, we haven't," Dinah snapped as she yanked the oxygen mask from Eric's hand.

"It was a slight tap," Eric said defensively.

"And you didn't stop to see if you'd damaged my car, or injured me," Dinah argued back as she slipped the pediatric-size oxygen mask over Bryce's face and turned on the emergency tank Eric had brought.

"I was in a hurry...emergency." Eric popped the stethoscope earpieces into his ears, then held up his hand to shush everybody. A moment later he looked up at Neil. "I think you could be right."

"Right?" Gabby choked out. "About what?"

"Neil thinks it might be TGV," Eric explained, "and at this point I have no reason to disagree because the symptoms fit. Things may turn out differently once we get the baby—"

"Bryce. Bryce Thierry Evans," Gabby interrupted.

"Thierry?" Eric questioned, looking downright shocked.

"Gavin was the father," Neil explained, not sounding as awkward as he could have.

Eric nodded, but didn't comment. "OK. Once we get *Bryce* to the hospital." He looked at Dinah. "You'll drive." Then he looked at Neil, a silent agreement passing between them. In the next instant he was gone, with Dinah soon to follow.

"What was that about?" Gabby asked, sliding to the edge of the bed.

"It's critical, Gabrielle. He'll do what he can to stabilize Bryce, and if it's TGV he'll probably do the balloon septostomy here in White Elk." Enlarging a small opening between the atria that is normally present at birth in order to let more oxygenated blood reach the body. "But we're going to have to send him down to the hospital in Salt Lake, where they can do more tests, as well as the follow-up surgery to reconnect the arteries normally."

"And you think it's TGV, Neil?"

"I'm afraid I do, Gabrielle. And I'm so sorry."

"Then I've got to go," she whispered. "Because when Eric does the septostomy, Bryce might not…" She stopped, unable to say the word.

"He's a good surgeon. Trust me on that. Eric will do everything humanly possible to take care of Bryce."

"I do trust you, Neil. And I trust Eric. But somehow you've got to get me there. Bryce can't go through this alone."

"I'll get you there," he promised.

Gabby glanced at Angela. "Come with me," she said. "I don't want you here alone."

Angela went on ahead, gathering blankets and rain gear, as Neil helped Gabby dress and get ready for the trip. "What if Bryce doesn't make it?" she choked as he pulled a sweater over her arms."

"He will, Gabrielle. Like I said, Eric is the best. If I had a baby who needed surgery, he'd be the only one I'd let do it."

"But sometimes the best isn't good enough."

"And sometimes it is." He pulled her into his arms and kissed her lightly on her forehead. "This time you have to trust that it is."

CHAPTER NINE

HUDDLED in the truck seat, squeezed between Angela and Neil, and wrapped so tightly in a cashmere blanket that her head was the only thing visible, Gabby didn't want to think about anything. It was too painful, too frightening. All these months connected to her son, and now she couldn't feel that connection any more. She couldn't feel anything. It was all gone, and it almost seemed like it had never been there at all. It was like those months had suddenly turned into a haze where everything was fast fading from her memory.

"Are you warm enough?" Neil asked her.

"Fine," she lied. Because nothing anyone could do would take the chill away. It was the cold, harsh iciness of fear that couldn't be quelled with a blanket, or ten blankets, or even a blast of heat from the truck's heater.

"And you, Angela. How are you doing?"

"I'm fine," she said, her voice on the edge of a quiver.

"Are you comfortable, Gabrielle?" he asked.

"Fine," she lied again. In truth, she was miserable, but not in the physical sense. It was as if her body didn't matter in all this. She'd given birth a little over an hour ago but the emotional pain had far outdistanced the physical pain of it. "Should you call Eric again?"

"We talked to him just a minute ago. They haven't reached the hospital yet."

"But I need to know about Bryce. I need to hear Eric tell me that Bryce is still…" She bit down hard on her bottom lip to keep herself from crying, as Angela reached to take her hand. Gabby knew that Bryce needed her to be strong for him, and that's what she had to do, no matter how hard that was right now. There would be plenty of time for the emotions later on. "I just need to know."

Neil hit speed dial, then handed the phone to Gabby. "How is he?' she whispered, fighting against the tremble in her voice as Eric answered.

"Fighting, Gabby. He's a strong little boy, and he's fighting like hell."

"Can I talk to him, Eric? He needs to hear my voice."

Neil glanced over at Gabby, and smiled, while she waited for Eric to give her the go-ahead. She found a brave smile to return to him. "It's not silly," she said. "He knows my voice."

"I know it's not silly. In fact, I'm pretty sure he's waiting to hear from you."

A look of hope flashed across her face. "Do you think so? Do you really think so?"

"The bond hasn't broken because he's not in your arms right now, Gabrielle. So, yes, I really think so."

"Neil, I'm so glad you're here. I don't think I could go through this without you." She squeezed Angela's hand. "You, too. And don't you worry. Things are going to go better with you when your time comes. And we'll deliver your lit-tle…baby in the hospital."

"You know what it is?" Angela asked.

Gabby nodded. "Do you want to?"

"Not yet."

Gabby actually laughed. "Well, in case you're curious, I have a pair of baby bootees for you in my bag. When you want to know, find them. See what the color is."

"You shouldn't be worrying about me right now, Gabby," she said.

"Of course I should." She squeezed Angela's hand again, then leaned her head against Neil's shoulder. Fatigue was setting in. "Just, please, don't go into labor early the way I did, because I'm really not up to a delivery today."

"But she's so stubborn she'd have had a go at it anyway," Neil said, the affection in his voice so clear that even Angela heard it. Neil was brushing his thumb across Gabby's cheek when Eric finally told her the phone was in place and that she could say a few words to Bryce.

Gabby took a deep breath, straightened in the seat, then let her breath back out, slowly bracing herself for the most important words she'd ever spoken in her life. It was time to step up and be the support her baby needed, just the way Neil had stepped up to be the support she needed. She looked at Neil for a moment to find the calm reassurance she always found in him. Then she spoke. "Bryce, I know this isn't the way we had things planned, but you've got to trust me. The very best doctors in the whole world are taking care of you now, and very soon you'll be feeling much better. Mommy's on her way, Bryce. I promise, Mommy will be there when you need me." She swiped at a stray tear running down her cheek, angry at herself for not being in better control. And for being so frightened. She was a doctor, after all. She'd delivered babies with the very same problem and seen the successes. Yet none of that did any good when it concerned her child. Her miracle baby. "I love you, Bryce. I love you so much, and I'll be there in a little while. We're going to get through this together. You've got to believe me, Bryce. We're going to get through this together. Be strong for Mommy."

Gabby clicked off the phone, then scooted back down in the seat, and cocooned herself even tighter in the blanket, more emotionally exhausted than before. "I always let my patients know the risks associated with pregnancy, and I try to prepare them in case something like this happens. But I never, *ever* prepared myself, and I refused to let myself think about it because this may be my one and only chance to have a baby. I suppose I wanted it so badly I blocked out common sense."

"It's normal, Gabrielle. Nobody wants to focus on the negatives. Pregnancy can be such a happy time, with so much to look forward to, so not thinking in terms of the things that could go wrong is the easiest thing to do. And, in my opinion, the best. I mean, suppose you'd spent every day worrying? Suppose you went over the checklist of everything that could go wrong rather than looking forward to all the things that could go right, the way you did? All that stress could have made things…"

"Worse?" she snapped. "Do you really believe things could have turned out worse?"

Angela took hold of her hand again, but didn't say a word.

"Yes," he said, his voice grave. "They could have, and deep down you know that. Bryce is alive, which gives him a chance. And with so many people fighting for him—" Before he could finish, the cell phone jingled, and she automatically clicked on. It was Eric telling her they'd arrived at the hospital, safe and sound, that they were en route to the surgery. "We're going to do some preliminary tests first, get some X-rays, type and cross-match him for a transfusion if we need one. If I have your consent."

"Of course you do. Anything at all…just do it." As Eric was signing off, Neil swerved to avoid a crater in the road, then swerved again to miss a rock that had slid down the hill. The rain had all but stopped, but the water was still on the rise. Not fast, but steady. Making the road slick with mud, and littered with so many blind obstructions that Neil's knuckles were white from gripping the steering wheel so hard.

Gabby saw this, saw the strain on his face as they slowed to ford a rivulet crossing over the road. It was deep, up to the bottom of the truck door—Angela's truck. It was a four-wheel drive, high-rider, thank God for small miracles. Otherwise they wouldn't have gotten though, and she wouldn't be able to kiss Bryce before he went into surgery.

And she had to kiss him. In fact, that was the only thing on her mind, the only thing she focused on until they reached the hospital.

Then finally, after the longest ride of her life, they were there. And it was a sight she'd never expected. Dozens of people were standing in water halfway up to their knees, filling sandbags, while dozens of other people placed the bags around the foundations of the hospital to hold back the rising waters. Yellow rain slickers everywhere, rain boots, umbrellas of every color and size… Those who weren't involved in bagging sand were taking hot coffee to the ones who were, and a temporary aid station had been set up on a makeshift wooden platform so people could get up out of the water for a while.

As Neil came to a stop, it was like all the workers gathered there came to a stop too, and turned to look at them as he helped Angela from the truck first, and gestured to an attendant with a wheelchair for her, then went back to help Gabby, literally scooping her up into his arms and carrying her inside. No protests. Once in the door, another one of the volunteers rushed forward with a wheelchair, but Neil refused it, still holding Gabby close, still running.

They were only part way through the lobby when her cell phone rang, and as she answered it she saw Eric running toward the front of the building to greet them, cell phone to his ear. Rather than talking into it, though, he simply stuffed it into his pockets and shouted, "Gabby, what blood type are you?"

She had to think for a moment. She knew, but it had escaped her.

But Eric didn't miss a beat. Before she could answer, he shouted, "Because Bryce has a rare blood type, and I want to have a unit of blood ready before we take him into surgery."

"Rare?" she asked.

"AB negative."

Meaning well less than one percent of the population had this blood type. And she did not. So that was Gavin's type.

Neil stopped abruptly. "That was the one thing Gavin and I had in common. I have type AB negative, too." He dropped Gabby into the wheelchair after all, and followed Eric back into the emergency department. Running.

"I'm not a medical person," Janice Laughlin said, stepping up behind Gabby and taking hold of the wheelchair handles, "but I guess that answers a lot of questions. Eric said he's never seen Neil as grumpy as he's been lately, and I'm guessing that's the reason."

"That's the reason," Gabby said, feeling scared, and dejected, and so many other things she couldn't even identify.

"I'm pretty sure he loves you."

"Maybe he does, but will it matter?"

"Time will tell, Gabby. Time will tell. But in the meantime, let's go down to the waiting area while my brother does the surgery. Laura's come in to sit with you, too, by the way."

Good friends, Gabby thought. Very good friends, and she didn't want to lose them. But right now everything she loved, everything she cared for was slipping away from her and she didn't know how to hang on.

As the surgery prep took place, Gabby stayed secluded in a private cubicle in the surgery department. Janice and Laura stayed with her. So did Angela, who was resting in a bed that had been brought in for her. Janice's daughter, Debbi, was valiantly minding all the children—Eric's twins as well as Laura's three—so the women could stay by Gabby's side. She loved them for that, but she wished Neil was there, being the support her friends were.

Neil never came in, though, and Gabby was sure the strain of it all was getting to him. She couldn't blame him for staying away from her, especially now that the secret was out. But she did so want his company. More than wanting him with her, though, she desperately hoped he was with Bryce. In her heart, she thought he was. Even though he'd been put through the emotional wringer by all this, she truly didn't believe that he'd walk away. The man she…loved simply wouldn't do that.

Oddly enough, it was Dinah who'd agreed to go into surgery with Eric. But not before she took Gabby to a bed in a private room and allowed her a few moments alone with her son. "You're a beautiful, strong little boy, Bryce," she whispered, fighting back the tears threatening to spill. "You're going to get through this just fine, then we'll start our life together and forget all this happened." But could she forget the parts that involved Neil? Because, she was afraid she might have to.

For the next few minutes Gabby sang lullabies, and hugged and kissed her baby. Then, all too soon, Dinah came to take him. "I'm sorry, Gabby, but it's time."

She didn't want to let him go, so she clung a little harder. "Gabby?"

Gabby nodded. "I know," she whispered, giving her baby one last kiss. "I love you, Bryce," Gabby whispered, then handed him over to Dinah.

When Bryce was gone, and Gabby was alone, she dropped her head back into the pillow and finally let the tears flow. "I really made a mess of things," she told Laura, who came in immediately.

"I heard."

"Everybody has, haven't they?" And by now Neil had to feel so humiliated…she just couldn't bear the thought of it.

"Nobody's judging you, Gabby. We know that Neil and Gavin had problems, but you must have known Gavin in a way that no one here did, and maybe, in time, that will be a good thing for Neil. For all of us, because we'd like to have better memories of him."

"If Neil ever speaks to me again once we get through this crisis."

"He will. But he may need some space for a while, so he can figure it out."

"I just don't know…"

"Do you love him?" Laura asked. She was fussing over Gabby, which Gabby didn't want but didn't have the strength to refuse.

"If I did, would it be enough for him?"

"Sometimes love is all there is. Be patient with yourself, and with Neil."

Gabby took the drink of water Laura poured for her, then slumped back against the pillows again. "But what if he never speaks to me again?"

"If he wants a relationship with his nephew, he will."

"That's the thing, isn't it? *If* he wants…"

"He's not heartless, Gabby. Hurt, maybe. But give him some time and distance, and he'll eventually do the right thing."

Of course he would. She knew that with all her heart. Neil was a kind, decent man. But even kind, decent men met their breaking point, and she'd practically slapped him in the face with his. "I just want this to be over, so I can have Bryce sent up to Salt Lake for the other surgery. Nothing else really matters."

"Would you come back?"

"Honestly, I don't know any more."

"Do you really think you can leave here and never look back?" Laura asked. "Because you have a life here. Friends, people who care. And that's not so easy to walk away from."

"No, it's not. And I do want the two of us to settle here. It's a wonderful little town, and I love the people. It's a perfect place to raise a child, and I've been happy, even though I haven't been here long. But…"

"Then stay here, Gabby. Settle down. Face your problems with some help from your friends. Raise your son."

"How can I do that?"

"You know what? Now's not the time to make any decisions. In fact, no decisions at all until you're thinking better. OK? So, since we're not talking about that now, do you want to hear the latest town gossip about how Eric hit Angela's sister's car and just drove off? And she chased him all the way to the hospital. I heard that the sparks are flying between those two, and not in a sexual way, if you know what I mean."

Small towns. She dearly loved this one, even with its gossip. If only there was a way she and Bryce could stay here.

Neil, standing concealed in a private cubicle across the hall from Gabby, watched her. She wasn't sleeping, even though her eyes were closed. She would never sleep while Bryce was in surgery. And if she were in any condition, she would have wanted to be in that surgery, inches away from her son, watching over him.

Which was what he had to do now. He'd been there through the preliminary tests, been there when they'd prepped Bryce for surgery. But he'd been torn, because he'd wanted to be with Gabrielle, too. Bryce needed him more, though, and there was no choice. "I'm going to gown up," he said quietly from the entry to her cubicle.

"Have you been with him?" She didn't yet open her eyes.

"Yes," he said simply. "I've been with him through everything so far."

The tears sliding down her cheeks broke his heart.

"I was hoping you were with him. You're the only one…" She finally raised her head to look at Neil, swiping at her tears as she did. "You and I, we're all he has. So I trust you to watch over my baby, Neil."

"I know you do, Gabrielle. I know you do." No more words were said, because it was time. He wanted to go to her, pull her into his arms and hold her until the pain went away. But the pain wasn't going to leave her until her baby was well. And his fear for that little boy…it was an agony like none he'd ever known.

"Neil?" Eric glanced up as Neil took his place next to the operating table.

As many times as he'd been in this very same position over the years—gowned and standing by to observe—this time seemed so daunting, almost foreign to him. Like he'd never really witnessed a surgery before. But, then, he'd never witnessed one in which he'd been so personally involved. "Just observing my…my nephew," he said. Bryce was so tiny, so helpless, lying there, as Eric cut into his chest. All these huge medical machines to sustain him and one small baby to sustain…it seemed so overwhelming. "How's he doing?"

"Good, so far. I think we got lucky…well, as lucky as we can get with a sick baby who has a heart defect. But it's a *simple* TGV, the best-case scenario with this, and I think after he has his next surgery his prognosis will be very promising for a bright and healthy future."

Neil was more relieved to hear that than he'd expected to be. A simple deviation always had a much better outcome than a complex one, and Bryce would get to live a normal life and do all the things all little boys did. "Gabrielle will be relieved to hear that," he said, trying to sound unaffected. But the truth was, he was already seeing Bryce a few years into the future, playing soccer, or baseball. Playing it with… Neil blanked the scene out of his head. It was too cozy, and he wanted to be involved in the boy's life. Wanted to be the one playing soccer or baseball with him. But he'd been making such a mess of things with Gabrielle, even after she'd done everything humanly possible to make things right for him, to make things better. So, in the end, would she have him? Or would she decide it wasn't worth the effort after all?

"Neil, I had no idea the baby was your nephew," Eric commented.

Fallon, who was assisting in the surgery, looked up at Neil, but said nothing. Dinah, who'd agreed to be the other assisting nurse, however, did comment. "You have the same eyes," she said.

Henry Gunther, the anesthesiologist, who'd literally been brought in by boat due to the flooding, glanced at Neil over the top of his glasses for a moment, glanced down at the baby, nodding. "Yep, same eyes," he agreed. "You going to marry Dr Evans? I heard that you two…"

"Is there anybody who hasn't heard?" Neil snapped.

"Probably not," Eric said as he tied off a small vessel and extended his hand to Dinah for a clamp. Dinah handed it to him. For just a fraction of a second Eric took his eyes off his surgical field and glanced across the table at her. Her eyes caught that glance, and held it almost defiantly until he returned his full attention to his patient.

"Small towns, Neil," he continued. "You know how it is. So, how's Gabrielle doing? It's been a rough day on her, physically and emotionally, and I'm sure she's feeling the effects right now."

"She's strong." He tried to sound disengaged, but as he looked at the bag of blood flowing into Bryce's vein—blood from his own vein—he knew he wasn't disengaged in any way, and could never be. In fact, he was more engaged here than he'd ever been in his entire life. To Bryce, to Gabrielle... "And I'm pretty damned stupid."

Dinah glanced up, first at Eric, then at Neil. "Angela told me you love Gabby, but you're not doing a very good job of it. But you're allowed to be a little stupid for a while, because people in love usually do something stupid along the way, don't they? I mean, who in this room hasn't been stupid in love?"

"Great. Even the out-of-towners know," Neil huffed out. "And here I was, living under the delusion that there were still a few people who hadn't yet gotten themselves caught up in the story of how Neil fell in love with the woman who had his brother's baby?"

Everyone in the operating theater chuckled. "No one ever claimed life in White Elk was dull," Fallon commented as she pulled the suture tray over, meaning the surgery was nearing its end.

Neil took a step closer to the operating table, and saw that Bryce had pinked up quite nicely. In part, that was due to him being ventilated by Henry Gunther, and in part because the blood was flowing better to Bryce's entire body now. It was something Gabrielle should have seen, had she been physically able. Something he would describe for her. "So, everybody knows how I feel about Gabrielle?" he asked, suddenly embarrassed that Gabrielle's friends had recognized his feelings for her even before he'd admitted it to himself, let alone to her.

"Everybody," everyone in the theater said in unison.

"So much for privacy," he snapped.

"Privacy?" Eric exclaimed. "You had all the privacy you needed when you lived in California. And you hated it. Remember? In fact, you were the one who convinced me that the charm of a small town like White Elk was just what I needed."

Neil ignored Eric's comment about small towns because Eric was right. "Have you made any arrangements to get Bryce out to Salt Lake City?"

"Rose Kelly is working on it. Last I heard, there's no place for miles for the helicopter to set down, so we'll have to be creative."

"But Bryce will be fine here for a while?" Now he was sounding like a worried parent because, as a doctor, he knew the answer to that question. Bryce would be fine here for quite a while. Right now, though, he couldn't reach down deep enough to find the doctor in him, when his feelings for that baby were all over the place.

Eric glanced over at Neil. "You should go be with Gabrielle now. She needs you. And you need her."

One last look at Bryce, and Neil walked out of the operating room. He dumped his surgical gown, mask and hat into the hamper outside the door, and turned to leave the area, but Gabby was standing in the doorway. More like leaning against it. Pale. Weak. Tired. And fighting with everything she had in her to be there.

"How is he?" she asked.

The worry on her face was plain. "You shouldn't be here, Gabrielle. You're not strong enough yet."

"Where else could I be?"

"Back in bed. Resting."

"But I wanted to find out. All I've been getting are the vague reports they call out from surgery. You know, 'It's going as well as can be expected.' 'Your baby is stable.'" She slumped a little harder against the door frame and Neil immediately sprang forward to support her, to wrap his arms around her and hold her up. "How is he, Neil? You were in there, you saw him. So, how is my son?"

"He's pink."

"Pink?"

"You know, pink, the way a baby should be."

"Pink," she said, leaning her head into his chest and sniffling. "My baby is pink."

"It's a simple TGV, Gabrielle. Eric said he's in good shape and his prognosis is promising."

She nodded, but didn't speak.

"And they're getting ready to close, so you should be able to see him in a little while."

"I'm glad you were with him, Neil. Somehow, I'm sure he knew that. I was in there," she whispered, then sighed in relief. "I *was* in there. Through you."

Touched, and choking back his own tears, Neil cleared his throat. "Look, you need to get back in bed. Eric will come and let you know when you can see Bryce."

"Where are you going?" she asked.

"Other patients. I have…other patients to see." That was a lie. But right now he just couldn't deal with this. There were too many emotions, too many memories. And he couldn't sort them out and, at the same time, be around Gabrielle, because Gabrielle clouded his judgment to the point where she was the only thing he could feel. The only thing he could see. Right now, he had to have objectivity and clear thinking. Because he loved her, and loved that little boy.

But would it be enough to get him past his feelings about Gavin?

Neil signaled to one of the nurses at the other end of the hall. "Please see to it that Dr Evans gets back to her room." Then he turned and walked away. Never looked back. Wouldn't look back, because if he did, he couldn't walk away. And right now, walking away was the only thing he could do.

"Are you sure you're up to this?" Eric asked Gabby.

"It's only a helicopter ride. I'll be fine." The surgery had ended twenty-four hours ago, and she'd spent almost every hour since then either holding Bryce or sitting next to his crib, counting fingers and toes, singing lullabies, kissing his chubby pink cheeks, just watching him and falling more and more in love.

Outside, the flood waters were receding, but not significantly. Activity had died down at the hospital, though. People weren't flowing in with the current as they had only a day ago because they were back home now, trying to make sense of the damages and salvage whatever they could. Walt Graham had finally wandered in, complained that he'd made a wasted trip as Gabby had already delivered. One by one, every friend she'd made in White Elk had come in to see her, and with the flooding still going on outside, for some of them it hadn't been an easy trip in. But she'd had a steady parade of visitors who made her feel so loved, and so much a part of something wonderful.

If home was where the heart was, in just a few short weeks she'd found home. But there was another heart to consider— one that wasn't hers, or Bryce's. That was the heart she would not break no matter what happened. All the hours with Bryce, all those hours holding him and being thankful for everything she had…that's when she'd made her decision. If Neil wanted her, she would stay. If he didn't, she would leave and allow him to have his life here without the constant reminder of his brother. It would be a sacrifice, but not too great a sacrifice if it made Neil whole again.

Besides, even though home was where the heart was, her heart was with Bryce and wherever they were together, that would be her home.

She only hoped, and prayed, that Neil would be part of that.

Gabby hadn't seen Neil, though. Neither had she heard from him. It hurt, but she was dealing with it the best way she could.

"Well, Fallon's going along to look after both you and Bryce," Eric said. "And I'll be in touch as soon as you land. The hospital is on alert, and Dr James Galbraith will be standing by to assume Bryce's care. So, you're good to go."

"Dr Galbraith is good?"

"I'd trust my twins to him."

Knowing that made her feel better. She was anxious for this trip, anxious to have Bryce in the hospital where he would have his next surgery, anxious for his recovery so they could start a normal life together. Still, she'd wanted…no, she'd hoped…Neil would stop by, wish her luck, check on Bryce. Anything. That simply wasn't to be the case, though. So she hugged Eric, climbed into the back of the ambulance and took a seat next to Fallon, then prepared herself for the trip up to the top of the middle Sister, where her medical transport awaited.

An hour later, she climbed out of the ambulance that had picked them up in Salt Lake City, and stepped back as a flurry of medical activity swooped in over Bryce. He was whisked straight away to the NICU—neonatal intensive care unit—not because he was in critical condition but as a precaution, while

Gabby was left behind to tend to the admittance chores like paperwork, consents and insurance.

"Father?" the admitting clerk asked, when she saw that section of the form had been left blank.

"No father," Gabby said. Then changed her mind. "Dr Gavin Thierry, deceased." He was Bryce's father and deserved that title, even posthumously.

"I'm sorry," the clerk said.

"So am I," Neil said, stepping up behind Gabby.

She spun to face him. "I didn't know you'd be here."

"Neither did I. Yesterday, when I left the hospital, I just drove. It took me hours to get out of the valley, taking all the high roads, and once I was finally out, I wasn't sure where I was going. So I came here. Took a room across the street at the hotel, and...waited."

"For Bryce."

"For you, Gabrielle. I wanted to see you."

"Your son's checked into the NICU now," the clerk interrupted. "You can go on up."

Gabby nodded her thanks to the woman, and started to head for the elevator. But halfway there she stopped, and turned back to Neil. "Are you coming?"

"Do you want me?"

"He's your nephew, Neil. He has your blood running through his veins. You have a right to be here." He had a right, but she desperately wanted him to have the need to be here, and right now she didn't know if that was the case, or if he'd come out of some kind of misplaced loyalty or obligation. "And I won't keep you out of his life, if you want to be in it."

He didn't speak as he stepped onto the elevator with her, or as he rode up to the fourth floor. And when the door opened, he stepped out without saying a word. But when Gabby gowned up and headed for the NICU, Neil said, "Tell him I'm here, and that I love him."

"Do you?" Gabby asked, not to be contentious but more because she wanted to know the answer.

"None of this has been easy, Gabrielle. Not for either of us. But whatever's happened, it has nothing to do with Bryce. He's an amazing little boy who's fighting his way through a tough situation, and he's going to need all the love he can get for a while."

"Only for a while? Because if that's your condition, then maybe you shouldn't be here. Because my son…Gavin's son…needs and deserves more than only your conditional love. He needs it strong, and he needs it forever. And if you can't give it to him that way, go back to your hotel, or back to White Elk. Or go anyplace you want to go so long as it's not here."

Gabby spun away and went though the NICU doors. Her hands were shaking. She wanted to cry. And scream. And kick the wall. Most of all, she wanted to go back outside and tell Neil that she loved him and she wanted him in her life…in Bryce's life. But on her terms, which were forever. When she looked back through the doors, though, he was gone. Beyond that, she couldn't think because she was rushed into the NICU for her first ten-minute visit, top of the hour, every hour thereafter.

Bryce looked so helpless, lying there in the crib, hooked to oxygen, hooked to an IV. She needed to hold him, needed to feel the intimate bond she'd had with him before his birth, but that had been breached and she couldn't. In this impersonal room full of machines and other worried parents, there was no place to whisper the things to him she'd whispered over the months, or to sing him the lullabies. But she touched him—laid her fingers on his tiny chest and felt him breath for those ten minutes. It wasn't nearly enough, but she was grateful. Because when she looked at her son lying there, sound asleep and oblivious to all the things causing her so much pain, she saw a miracle. Seven months ago, when she'd learned she was pregnant, she'd known it was a miracle. And now that Bryce was here, and on his way to being healthy, she was filled with overwhelming gratitude to the man Neil hated. So maybe that situation couldn't be rectified. As much as she wanted it to be, she just didn't know. "What will be, will be," she whispered to Bryce, as she kissed him on the forehead just as her visit was up. "But no matter what, Mommy loves you and that will never change."

CHAPTER TEN

"I THOUGHT you might like some hot chocolate." Neil handed over a plastic cup, and sat down next to Gabrielle, who was stretched out in bed, staring at the wall. The hospital had checked her into a private room, more as a guest than a patient, partly as a medical privilege, partly because of her condition.

"I didn't know you were still here." She took the cup, clutching it like it was her life blood. She'd been so cold since she'd come here, so cold since she'd had to walk away from Bryce and leave him all alone in Intensive Care, and the warmth felt good on her fingers.

"I couldn't leave, Gabrielle. Right now, I'm as mixed-up as you are about how this will work out, but the one thing that I knew for sure was that I couldn't walk away from you and Bryce."

"I don't want you to leave, Neil." Gabby sucked in a sharp breath, held it for a moment, then let it out. "If that's what you think you have to do, I won't stop you. I'll honor your wishes, whatever they are. But just so you'll know, my wish is that you'd be part of our family. Bryce and me. You and me. *Especially* you and me."

Neil laughed. "You never mince words, Gabrielle. That was one of the first things that attracted me to you. When I was married to Karen, I never knew where I stood. With you, I always do."

"Life's too short to play games, and I think I'm only just now coming to understand what that really means." It was a bit of her father's wisdom she'd taken to heart a long, long time ago. "My dad always said that when the opportunity arises, grab it and hold on for dear life, because you might never get that opportunity again."

"He was a wise man. I wish I could have met him."

"I wish you could have, too. You would have liked him. And I think he would have liked you."

"Maybe I'll get to know him through his grandson."

"Is that what you really want, Neil? Because while he's Bryce Evans's grandson, he's also Gavin Thierry's son, and that's never going to change."

"Tell me about my brother, Gabrielle. You know things about him I need to know."

Yes, he did need to know. Finally. She took a deep breath to brace herself. "We met at a medical seminar in Chicago, about nine months ago, as it turns out. It was also just a few weeks after I'd buried my father, and I was so…alone. My dad was, quite literally, the only person I had in the world. No other relatives, except a few distant cousins. We were very close, probably closer than most fathers and daughters because he was the one who raised me. So, pretty much, it was just the two of us. Anyway, I wasn't back to work yet, was pretty sure I didn't want to return to that particular practice when I was ready to work again, and I needed something to keep me occupied until I figured out what I wanted…I was pretty lost. So I went to a pediatrics seminar and figured that since I deliver babies, it might do me some good to learn some advances in pediatrics."

"And that's where you met Gavin."

Gabby nodded. "He was a lecturer. Brilliant, so passionate in his love of pediatrics. I think I fell a little in love with him when I heard him speak, because I'd never heard anyone with such excitement about his work. He lectured on operating a small-town pediatric practice, talked about how important pediatric specialties were to the more rural or isolated areas, and outlined ways to get better service to those areas. Maybe the most important thing he did was tell those of us who came to his lecture to consider small-town practice when we were weighing our options, and not to write it off too quickly. He was brilliant, Neil. People approached him afterwards and told him that he'd given them something to think about."

"Really?"

Gabby nodded. "He was respected. Well researched, well-spoken. All that, and he was nice to me when I desperately needed someone to be nice. He…he distracted me from the things I didn't want to think about yet. One thing led to another. So at a time when I was lower than I'd ever been in my life, Gavin and I connected. I might have been a little in love, or maybe a better way to put that is infatuated. But it wasn't permanent. Wasn't meant to be anything more than it was, and we knew that after a little while. But for a couple of days we were two people who were both going through some lows, trying to pick each other up."

"He was going through some lows?"

Gabby nodded. "He didn't say anything about it, but you could see it in his eyes." Eyes that were so much like Neil's. And she'd seen that same distance in his eyes, too.

She shifted in bed, settled back more into her pillows,

raised the head a little. And shut her eyes, trying to picture Gavin. Funny thing was, all she saw was Neil. They really didn't look so much alike, except the eyes. Bryce's eyes. "It didn't turn into a real relationship, Neil. We were careful, even though no one would have ever believed I could have a child, but apparently Bryce was meant to be. I wanted Gavin to be part of his son's life, if he wanted to. I was going to give him that opportunity."

"As possessive as you are about Bryce, didn't that scare you?"

"It did. I mean, he could have wanted full custody, or partial custody. He might have wanted to have influence in ways I wouldn't approve of. There were a lot of risks, letting him know."

"So why, ultimately, did you decide to do it when he probably would have never found out?"

"Because it was the right thing to do. Bryce had a right to his father, and his father had a right to Bryce." Overhead, the hospital light seemed especially harsh shining in her face, and she reached up to shut it off. Then she twisted to have a better look at Neil. "Everything was going so well in my life…I was having the baby I never thought I'd have, and falling in love with the man I thought I'd never meet. It was so perfect, and I didn't want it to end. But that day in the hospital, when I saw Gavin's name on the plaque…how could anyone be prepared for a situation like that? How could anyone even know what to do? Gavin had hurt you, and here I was, having his baby and falling in love with you." She stopped. The words had run out. There was nothing more to say that he hadn't already heard. So now it was up to Neil to make the next move. And there were so many ways this could go, it frightened her to the very core because she wanted to be a family with him. The three of them. Living in White Elk. Happy.

Only she didn't know if Neil could do that. So, now was the moment of reckoning. Her destiny laid out before her, and the choice was Neil's.

"Gavin and I were…at the time he died we were almost getting along again. He'd changed. I saw it after he'd come back from his medical seminar. He was…calm. Maybe a little more contented. And that was something I'd never seen in him before. Ever. But he'd called me and we'd talked a few times. He'd told me how sorry he was for breaking up my marriage. He, um…he begged for my forgiveness and I told him I wasn't ready yet, but maybe sometime in the future. It was the best I could do."

"That's good," Gabrielle said, her hopes growing even though she was trying to hold them back.

"Not good, but better. There were too many hard feelings to clear up in a matter of days or weeks. And I think he understood that."

"Maybe that was the sadness I saw in him. The regret for what he'd done. We all make mistakes, and maybe he was at a point where he was realizing that his biggest mistake was losing his brother."

Neil shrugged. "Maybe. But we'll never know, will we?"

"What we know is that the man I met wasn't the man who stole your wife. Something changed him, Neil, and while we'll never know what that was, it would be nice to think that Gavin's desire to have a relationship with you again caused the change. Honestly, I think he found his heart and his happiness through his medicine and, perhaps, that's where the change in him started. And you know what? I think his lecture was about White Elk, even though he didn't mention it by name. It was his passion, like it's yours."

"Karen and I weren't getting along when Gavin stepped in. She was such a…mistake. More like a lapse in sound judgment. And, to be honest, I didn't miss her when she was gone."

"But did you miss Gavin?"

"Not for a while. I remember telling him something to the

effect that I never wanted to see him again…something about not crossing his path until hell froze over." He cringed. "It was reactionary, but I had a right to my reactions. And not because of Karen. She wasn't even significant in the matter. My wife was poison. She would have destroyed me, destroyed my career. And after I'd found out they'd been having an affair, I laughed at Gavin for being so gullible, told him he was welcome to her." Neil shook his head. "And the hell of it was, I never knew why they did it. Karen was easy to figure out. She was a child who got bored with her toys easily. But Gavin?"

"It could have been something complicated like a deep-rooted jealousy left over from childhood—like he perceived you were the favored one, or something as simple as being hurt that his father knew you were following in his footsteps, but didn't live long enough to know that Gavin was, too. It's hard to say what caused him to do what he did, and speculating is a waste of time because we'll never know. But the way you reacted…you said what you said because you were hurt. Gavin wouldn't have held that against you. I mean, there aren't rules governing a situation like that. But you rebuilt your life. Honorably. And in the end, even though you'll never have the answers you want, you'll have to make your life enough without those answers."

"It is enough. More than I ever thought I'd have, and I'm happy. Probably happier than Gavin ever was, and I'm sorry for that. Truly, deeply sorry."

Tears of pain trickled down her cheeks, and she swiped at them with the back of her hand. "The man I met had regrets, Neil. I saw that in him and I wish now I'd asked him." Yet how could she have anticipated, then, how her future would be eternally entwined with Gavin's? Or his brother's? Or his son's?

"Gavin and I, we'd agreed to meet. After months, I'd finally said yes, stipulating that the first meeting be on neutral ground somewhere other than White Elk. We'd have lunch, talk. We'd agreed to one step at a time. Gavin wanted to go faster, I wanted to be cautious. But we were going to sit down together and see if we could find a starting point." He swallowed hard. "I didn't know he changed his will to leave everything to the hospital pediatrics ward. He was atoning for what he'd done in the past, I think."

"Yes, I think he was."

"Even with all his faults, Gavin was a brilliant doctor. I would have liked to have heard his lecture in Chicago."

"Would you like to read my notes of it?"

He nodded, but didn't speak for a moment. Then, finally, "Gavin and I had a long way to go to make up. He said he understood that, and was willing to do whatever he had to. He was sincere, Gabrielle. I know he was sincere."

"Because he was a changed man," she said.

"Yes, I think he was. And I don't suppose I would have known how much if you hadn't…"

He cleared his throat and shut his eyes for a moment. Thinking. Processing. Trying to put it all together. The agony on his face was so strong it turned into her own agony. She could feel it. Feel the heavy burden he carried. If only there was something she could do, something more than listening. But maybe that's what he needed most. Maybe letting him unburden himself was the only thing she could do to truly help. So she waited quietly until he was ready to speak again, hoping he could feel her silent support.

"Anyway," he finally said, "Gavin wanted to see me and I had finally convinced myself it was a good thing. I wasn't looking forward to it, although I wasn't dreading it either. But I had a patient who went bad that morning and I couldn't leave the hospital. So I called Gavin, told him we'd have to reschedule, and that I'd call him in a day or so to see what we could arrange. Well, Gavin was insistent. He said he was coming to White Elk to see me, that he was ready to do it, and he had things to say that couldn't wait any longer. So he came to White Elk, and that's when…when he was killed. Traffic accident right before he got to the valley."

"Neil, I'm so sorry." Gabby scooted to the edge of the bed, dropped her legs over the side, then leaned forward and took Neil's hands in hers. "So sorry you two never had the chance to talk." She couldn't even begin to imagine what it would be like to be involved in a relationship that needed resolution as badly as Neil's and Gavin's had, and never have that chance. When she'd lost her dad, everything had been said between them. No resolution was necessary, because they'd expressed their love, fought their fights and forgiven each other along the way. Even thinking that something between them could have gone unresolved made her feel sad. For Neil, for Gavin. And for Bryce, because he was very much a part of this.

But more than ever it made her realize that she and Neil had a situation to resolve between the two of them, and that they couldn't let another day, another hour pass without saying all the things that needed saying.

"I know you can't go back and change things, and I'm sure you thought, like most of us do, that you have all the time in the world to make things right. It's just not like that, though. My little boy almost died yesterday, and that's the first time I've really understood how precious and short time is. Gavin was a good man. I knew him differently than you did, saw him in a way you'll never get to. But he was a good, kind man, and I have to think he learned from his mistakes and patterned himself after you. Because you're a good, kind man, too. His older brother…the best kind of example. He knew that, and I truly believe that hurting you was what made him sad. So maybe you didn't have enough time to make it right, but you would have, Neil. Given enough time, you two would have made up. He wanted to, and you wanted to."

"Maybe we would have. But I'll never know, will I?"

The truth was, he wouldn't. And that wasn't something she could fix. She could help him through it, though. Support him through the lows. If he would have her. If he would have Bryce. "I don't want to leave White Elk, Neil. I want to stay there and raise my son there. And I want to be happy there. When I first arrived, I didn't know what I wanted, or where I wanted to be. But I found everything...*everything* there, and I don't want to leave it. But I can't stay, if my being there makes you unhappy."

"You could never make me unhappy, Gabrielle. I knew that the first time I saw you in the dining room, being so deliberate about picking out the right table so you could see what you wanted to see. I'll admit I never expected to fall in love with someone quite so..."

"Pregnant?"

He chuckled. "That, too. But the word I'm looking for is perfect. Because you are." He took hold of her hand and pulled it to his lips, then kissed it tenderly. "I don't think I've mentioned this before, but you look beautiful when you're not pregnant. Of course, you're absolutely stunning when you're pregnant. Any chance that could happen again?"

"And that would mean?" It was definitely time to get her hopes up. In fact, they were so far up they were floating.

"About fifty or sixty years, if we're lucky."

"And you're good with Bryce being Gavin's son? Because that's something he'll have to know when it's time."

"I'm already crazy in love with him, so I'm good," he said. "As long as you let him call me Daddy."

"Daddy suits you. But I can't promise you other children, Neil. One was a miracle." Gavin's miracle to both Neil and her.

"One's perfect. So are ten."

"Ten?" she sputtered, slipping from the bed, going straight onto his lap and into his waiting arms. "You would want ten?"

"Or twelve. Or, like I said, one."

As their lips met, Gabby thought about that day she'd first come to White Elk, amazed by what a perfect town it was. The place, from Ben Gault's photos, that had stolen her heart. Her home, meant to be even before she'd recognized it. Yes, it was perfect. But not for the reasons she'd thought when she'd made the decision to spend a night there. White Elk was where her son had been born, where she'd met the man she'd love forever, where she'd found the dream of her heart. Those were the things that made it perfect. And made it home. "I love you, Dr Ranard," she said, resting her head on his shoulder, happier than she'd ever thought was possible.

"And I love you, Dr Evans. Want to snuggle up?" He pointed to the bed.

"Right here? I mean, I just had a baby, and..."

He laughed. "Snuggle, Dr Evans. *Only* snuggle."

"In that case, I'd love to snuggle with you, Dr Ranard. Every day, for the rest of my life."

EPILOGUE

Six months later

"HE's gained another pound." Neil picked up his son and held him high above his head, laughing. The adoption was final. Bryce Thierry Evans Ranard was his in every way and it was hard for either him or Gabby to imagine a time when this bouncing bundle of energy hadn't been the center of their lives.

"Eric said he's perfect. Everything checks out fine. Heart's good, lungs sound. Normal in every way. Oh, and I ran into Angela. She was there at the clinic with her baby…"

"Sarah," Gabby reminded him.

"With Sarah. Anyway, seeing Angela reminded me that we haven't had our honeymoon yet. So I was thinking that if we could find a babysitter…"

Gabby arched skeptical eyebrows. "I'm sensing a definite plot here, Bryce. Your father is up to something."

"I'm up to a short honeymoon," Neil said. After Bryce's second surgery, the three of them had settled in like a happy family, and the honeymoon had been forgotten. Tonight was the four-month anniversary of their marriage, though, and it was time for the two of them to get away. "And I've had a whole battalion of women volunteer to watch Bryce for a couple of days while we go up to Pine Ridge…couldn't get the honeymoon suite, though. It was already reserved by someone else. But we'll have a nice room anyway. Room service when we want it, lots of time alone…" Neil lowered Bryce, and looked him straight in the eye. "You may have to help me convince her," he said, grinning.

She took Bryce away from Neil. "You tell your father that your mother would love to have a honeymoon with him."

"Two whole nights," Neil reminded her.

"Two wonderful nights," she said, handing Bryce back to Neil, then picking up the bag she'd been hiding. "Shield his eyes," she said.

"Why?"

"Because he's too young to see this."

"Don't look, son," he said, laughing, as Gabrielle pulled a black, filmy nightdress out and waved it.

"Oh, and I'm the one who reserved the honeymoon suite, by the way. Already had several people ready to take care of Bryce, too." By all estimates, she had about another two months before her belly would start bulging again, and she wanted to take full advantage of that. Or, at least, two nights of it.

"Any chance we can stay away for a week?" he asked.

"With the way our medical practices are growing?" She waved the nightdress again, deliberately brushing it against his cheek. "Let's be glad we can have two nights, then promise to do it again in another month. Maybe try out a honeymoon suite at a lodge on one of the other Sisters."

"The practices are expanding, Bryce, because your mommy's a good doctor and women from everywhere are coming to see her."

"That's because your daddy turned his house on the hill into a women's clinic and birthing center." Her very own hospital, named The Three Sisters Women's Hospital. The Three Sisters who did, indeed, look after the people in their valley.

She and Neil had bought a modest little cottage on the edge of town, a perfect spot from which they could see all Three Sisters. Somehow she felt connected to them, like they'd watched over Bryce and protected him the way the legend had it. Like they'd brought her here in the first place so they could do just that.

Bryce's response was to gurgle out a baby bubble. Then laugh.

"But Mommy doesn't want to talk medicine right now," she said, tickling Neil's other cheek with the nighty. He was the perfect father. Devoted. Caring. Best of all, he didn't mind diaper duty. "But we will have to come home for a little while because Ben Gault is coming to town tomorrow afternoon. He's going to do a family photo of us." A family photo—her very own family. For her entire life, her family photo had been of two. But now, with three, then in a few more months with four…she still had to pinch herself sometimes to make sure it wasn't a dream.

"Ben Gault is going to interrupt my honeymoon? Couldn't we wait until he's here again in a couple of months?"

"We could, but I'll be showing."

"Showing what?" he asked.

She smiled warmly, and patted her belly.

"No!" he gasped.

"Yes," she whispered. "We might be on our way to the ten or twelve you wanted."

He snatched the black nightdress away from Gabrielle and

let it float to the floor. When it cascaded into a puddle at his feet, he smiled. "Well, then, I don't think you'll be needing this."

She bent and picked it up, then dropped it back into the bag, gave Bryce a kiss on the forehead and Neil a deep, lingering kiss on the lips. Afterwards, breathlessly…"I think you're right."

0410 Gen Std HB

MILLS & BOON

MAY 2010 HARDBACK TITLES

ROMANCE

Virgin on Her Wedding Night	Lynne Graham
Blackwolf's Redemption	Sandra Marton
The Shy Bride	Lucy Monroe
Penniless and Purchased	Julia James
Powerful Boss, Prim Miss Jones	Cathy Williams
Forbidden: The Sheikh's Virgin	Trish Morey
Secretary by Day, Mistress by Night	Maggie Cox
Greek Tycoon, Wayward Wife	Sabrina Philips
The French Aristocrat's Baby	Christina Hollis
Majesty, Mistress...Missing Heir	Caitlin Crews
Beauty and the Reclusive Prince	Raye Morgan
Executive: Expecting Tiny Twins	Barbara Hannay
A Wedding at Leopard Tree Lodge	Liz Fielding
Three Times A Bridesmaid...	Nicola Marsh
The No. 1 Sheriff in Texas	Patricia Thayer
The Cattleman, The Baby and Me	Michelle Douglas
The Surgeon's Miracle	Caroline Anderson
Dr Di Angelo's Baby Bombshell	Janice Lynn

HISTORICAL

The Earl's Runaway Bride	Sarah Mallory
The Wayward Debutante	Sarah Elliott
The Laird's Captive Wife	Joanna Fulford

MEDICAL™

Newborn Needs a Dad	Dianne Drake
His Motherless Little Twins	Dianne Drake
Wedding Bells for the Village Nurse	Abigail Gordon
Her Long-Lost Husband	Josie Metcalfe

0410 Gen Std LP

MAY 2010 LARGE PRINT TITLES

ROMANCE

Ruthless Magnate, Convenient Wife	Lynne Graham
The Prince's Chambermaid	Sharon Kendrick
The Virgin and His Majesty	Robyn Donald
Innocent Secretary...Accidentally Pregnant	Carol Marinelli
The Girl from Honeysuckle Farm	Jessica Steele
One Dance with the Cowboy	Donna Alward
The Daredevil Tycoon	Barbara McMahon
Hired: Sassy Assistant	Nina Harrington

HISTORICAL

Tall, Dark and Disreputable	Deb Marlowe
The Mistress of Hanover Square	Anne Herries
The Accidental Countess	Michelle Willingham

MEDICAL™

Country Midwife, Christmas Bride	Abigail Gordon
Greek Doctor: One Magical Christmas	Meredith Webber
Her Baby Out of the Blue	Alison Roberts
A Doctor, A Nurse: A Christmas Baby	Amy Andrews
Spanish Doctor, Pregnant Midwife	Anne Fraser
Expecting a Christmas Miracle	Laura Iding

0510 Gen Std HB

JUNE 2010 HARDBACK TITLES

ROMANCE

Marriage: To Claim His Twins	Penny Jordan
The Royal Baby Revelation	Sharon Kendrick
Under the Spaniard's Lock and Key	Kim Lawrence
Sweet Surrender with the Millionaire	Helen Brooks
The Virgin's Proposition	Anne McAllister
Scandal: His Majesty's Love-Child	Annie West
Bride in a Gilded Cage	Abby Green
Innocent in the Italian's Possession	Janette Kenny
The Master of Highbridge Manor	Susanne James
The Power of the Legendary Greek	Catherine George
Miracle for the Girl Next Door	Rebecca Winters
Mother of the Bride	Caroline Anderson
What's A Housekeeper To Do?	Jennie Adams
Tipping the Waitress with Diamonds	Nina Harrington
Saving Cinderella!	Myrna Mackenzie
Their Newborn Gift	Nikki Logan
The Midwife and the Millionaire	Fiona McArthur
Knight on the Children's Ward	Carol Marinelli

HISTORICAL

Rake Beyond Redemption	Anne O'Brien
A Thoroughly Compromised Lady	Bronwyn Scott
In the Master's Bed	Blythe Gifford

MEDICAL™

From Single Mum to Lady	Judy Campbell
Children's Doctor, Shy Nurse	Molly Evans
Hawaiian Sunset, Dream Proposal	Joanna Neil
Rescued: Mother and Baby	Anne Fraser

0510 Gen Std LP

MILLS & BOON

JUNE 2010 LARGE PRINT TITLES

ROMANCE

HISTORICAL

MEDICAL™

millsandboon.co.uk Community

Join Us!

The Community is the perfect place to meet and chat to kindred spirits who love books and reading as much as you do, but it's also the place to:

- Get the inside scoop from authors about their latest books
- Learn how to write a romance book with advice from our editors
- Help us to continue publishing the best in women's fiction
- Share your thoughts on the books we publish
- Befriend other users

Forums: Interact with each other as well as authors, editors and a whole host of other users worldwide.

Blogs: Every registered community member has their own blog to tell the world what they're up to and what's on their mind.

Book Challenge: We're aiming to read 5,000 books and have joined forces with The Reading Agency in our inaugural Book Challenge.

Profile Page: Showcase yourself and keep a record of your recent community activity.

Social Networking: We've added buttons at the end of every post to share via digg, Facebook, Google, Yahoo, technorati and de.licio.us.

www.millsandboon.co.uk